Polly plays her

Belmont

THE RIDGEWAY, MILL HILL

ET·VIRTUTEM·ET·MUSAS

LEARNING RESOURCES
CENTRE

Telephone: 020 8906 7270

Polly plays her Part

Anne-Marie Conway

USBORNE

For Callum and Freddy – my two brilliant boys!

First published in 2010 by Usborne Publishing Ltd., Usborne House,
83-85 Saffron Hill, London EC1N 8RT, England.
www.usborne.com

A CIP catalogue record for this book is available from the British Library.

JFMAMJJA OND/10   00591/1   ISBN 9781409520917
Printed in Reading, Berkshire, UK.

1
A New Show

"My name is Polly and I'm here today, to say my name in a rapping way!"

That's one of the games we play at Star Makers – the drama club I go to on Saturdays. It's called the rapping name-game and it's really cool, but if I was playing it right now I'd change the words and say:

"My name is Polly and I'm here tonight, sleeping at my dad's and ready for a fight!"

I didn't want to sleep at Dad's. But I didn't want to sleep at Mum's either. Maybe I could sleep somewhere in the middle, like at number 19. I swear no one believes me when I tell them that my mum and dad live only seven houses away from each other – Dad and Diane at

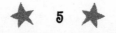

number 11 and Mum at number 25. Seven houses – or fifteen giant strides – or forty-eight pigeon steps (where you put one foot down exactly in front of the other, heel touching toe).

So I was sleeping round at Dad's. Or *not* sleeping as the case may be. It was impossible to get to sleep because the stupid baby was crying. Dad's *new* baby. Except he wasn't crying any more, he was screaming. It was so loud, Mum could probably hear him down the road at hers.

"Diane! I can't find his dummy!" Dad hissed from their bedroom. *"You know I'll never settle him without his dummy."*

I heard Diane get up and shuffle around the bed to the cot.

"Hang on a sec, Simon, I'll find it."

The screaming got louder. I could imagine the baby's face screwed up like an old tissue.

"Here it is, Jakey-boy," said Diane, in her

soppy *talking to the baby* voice. And the screaming stopped.

"It's like magic, you know," said Dad, yawning. "It's just like waving a magic wand."

I lay in bed for a bit longer, as the house grew quiet again, thinking about the magic wand *I'd* like to wave – the one that would get rid of Diane and *Jakey-boy* for good. After a bit, when I was sure Dad and Diane were asleep, I got up and turned on my new laptop. Dad bought me the laptop when he moved in here. It was supposed to make everything okay – leaving Mum, moving in with Diane, having a new baby. Like getting a new computer could make up for all of that!

The screen glowed in the dark as I pulled on an old sweatshirt and sat down ready to tap in my secret password. There were all sorts of sites Dad had forbidden me from going on, particularly social networking sites, but I wasn't that bothered about chatting to a bunch of

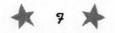

strangers anyway. I searched around for a bit until I found this game called **THWACKERS**, where you have to eliminate the bad guys before they eliminate you. I played for ages and by the time I logged off my score was so high I was third on the leader board.

"WELL DONE," the computer flashed. **"YOU HAVE SUCCESSFULLY ELIMINATED ALL YOUR ENEMIES!"**

Diane was making pancakes when I went down in the morning. Dad had told her once that I love pancakes and ever since then she makes them whenever I stay over.

"Morning, Polly," said Dad. "You look shattered. I hope Jakey didn't wake you. He couldn't find his dummy."

Jake was propped up in his highchair. As soon as he saw me he started to bang his plastic spoon on the tray and then he flung it on the floor and reached his arms out. He does that whenever anyone walks in, so it's not as if he

8

was especially happy to see *me* or anything.

"I'm going home to Mum's straight after breakfast," I said, sitting as far away from Jake and his sloppy breakfast as I could get. "She's taking me out to get new school shoes."

Dad glanced at Diane. "She didn't say anything about that," he said, frowning. "We were going to go down to the park later. Jakey's really looking forward to it, aren't you, Jakey?" He put his face right into Jake's and gave him a big slobbery kiss. Jake squealed in delight and banged his spoon even harder.

"He's only eight months old, Dad. I don't think he understands stuff like, *looking forward to things*. And anyway, I'm too old to *play* in the park."

"He looks forward to seeing *you*, Polly," said Diane, handing me a plate piled high with pancakes. "His eyes light up every time you walk in the room. You must've noticed. We *all* look forward to it," she added. "Don't we,

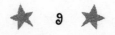

Simon?" Dad nodded but he didn't take his eyes off Jake, not for a second.

Diane's always saying nice things like that to try and get me to like her. Honestly, it's desperate. She goes on and on about my green eyes as if they're really special – and she says other stupid stuff like, "You're lucky being so slim, Polly," and, "Oh, I'd love to have black hair like yours, it's *so* dramatic!" She's really young – years younger than Mum – and she's got this crazy idea that we're going to end up best friends or something.

"I don't actually like pancakes any more," I said, pushing my plate away. "Can I have some cereal?"

Diane sighed and passed my pancakes across to Dad. I knew I was being stroppy but I didn't care. I'm always stroppy round at Dad and Diane's; *looking for a fight*, Dad says – but it's not like *I* started it!

I walked back home very slowly. Pigeon

steps – heel to toe, heel to toe. I passed number 13, then 15, 17, 19, 21 and 23. All the odd numbers. Maybe if we lived on the other side of the road where all the numbers were even my *life* might be a bit more even. I mean, everyone knows how totally *odd* it is to fall in love with someone who lives in the same street as you.

"Have you heard about Polly Carter's dad?" all the neighbours were saying when it happened. "He's only gone and moved in with Diane at number 11!"

I hung about outside Mum's for as long as I could. We weren't really going to get new school shoes – I just couldn't face spending the day with Dad and Diane. And I'm not too old to go to the park either; I'm only in Year Seven. It's just that whenever we go anywhere together, me, Dad, Diane and the baby, I know people are staring at us and whispering behind their hands.

"Poor Polly," they're probably saying. "Pushed aside to make way for The Great Baby Jake."

Suddenly the front door flew open and Mum came charging down the path.

"Hey, watch it!" I yelled, jumping out of the way just in time.

"Polly! What on earth are you doing here? You scared me half to death."

She was dressed up really smart in a dark-grey suit and high heels and she'd blow-dried her hair.

"You're supposed to be over at your dad's, aren't you? Oh never mind – listen, I can't stop. Make yourself something for lunch and I'll see you later."

She swept past me, her hair flying out behind her. I watched her all the way to the top of the road to see if she'd look back and wave or something, but she shot round the corner and disappeared. It was totally weird to see her all glammed up and rushing off so early in the morning. She's hardly been out since Dad left. She spends most of the time cleaning the house; scrubbing away for hours on end. And *I* spend most of the time tiptoeing around her as quietly as I can – doing my best to keep out the way.

It was almost the end of the Easter holidays and I felt as if I'd spent the whole break going up and down the road from Mum's to Dad's and back again. I let myself in and a massive ball of brown fur came hurtling down the stairs to greet me.

"Hello, Cosmo," I said, picking up my long-haired tabby cat. "At least *you're* pleased to see me." Cosmo snuggled into my arms and we walked down the hall towards the kitchen.

I stopped dead in the doorway, staring. The kitchen was a total mess. I'd only been gone for one night but it looked as if Mum hadn't cleared up for a year. There were plates piled up everywhere with bits of dried food and empty wine glasses all over the place. There was even a half-full bottle of champagne. I didn't remember her saying anything about a party, but it looked as if she'd had loads of people round. I'd never seen the kitchen in such a state.

I set about clearing up. Mum would only have a go if I left it. I spent ages sorting out the glasses and stacking all the dishes in the sink. I was just about to start washing up when the doorbell rang. I thought it might be Mum for a minute – that maybe she'd forgotten her keys – but it was the postman.

"Hello, love. Sign for this would you, pet?"

He thrust an important-looking letter at me addressed to Mum. I scribbled my name where he pointed and went back inside. I had a quick look through the rest of the mail and saw there was one letter for me – the letter I'd been waiting for *all* holiday! I left Mum's post by the

front door and sat down with Cosmo at the bottom of the stairs to open mine.

It was from Mandy Howell, my Year Seven form teacher, who runs Star Makers. She'd promised she was going to write to us while we were off school, but the days had trickled by with no sign of a letter. It was such a relief to see her funky handwriting on the envelope, full of twirls and curls. There were two sheets of paper inside; one addressed to Mum with all the boring details and one addressed to me. I read my one out loud to Cosmo.

Star Makers Drama Club

Dear Polly,

I hope you're having a fab holiday eating your way through a huge pile of Easter eggs! We've got a really exciting term coming up at Star Makers because it's time for a brand-new show!

Ever wondered what it would be like to be trapped inside your own computer with only a bunch of nasty viruses for company? Well you're about to find out when we start our new musical, CRASH!

There are loads of great parts, brilliant songs and dances, and we'll also be making some fantastic costumes and props.

Term starts next Saturday, 15th April. Same time – same place.

Look forward to seeing you there!

Mandy xxx

"*You'd* never get trapped inside a computer, would you?" I said to Cosmo, smiling for the first time in days. "You wouldn't fit for a start." I couldn't wait to get back to Star Makers. Something to look forward to at last!

Cosmo leaped off my lap suddenly as my phone began to vibrate in my jeans pocket. It was my new friend, Phoebe. I say *new* friend because Phoebe and I didn't get on at all when we first joined Star Makers. I was really jealous of her for some reason and it made me act like a total idiot. We kind of sorted things out at the end of last term and since then we've chatted on the phone a few times.

"Hi, Polly. Have you had your Star Makers' letter yet?"

"It's literally arrived this minute. I can't wait to get started."

"Me neither. It sounds brilliant, doesn't it? Hey, I wonder what colour Mandy's hair will be?"

"Well last time we saw her it was bright purple, wasn't it?"

"With yellow tips, don't forget," said Phoebe. "Listen, do you want to meet up later? My little sister's trying to compose a song on her recorder and if I don't get out soon I'll end up strangling her or something!"

"I'm sure it's not as bad as all that," I said,

giggling. I couldn't believe she was being so friendly and that she actually wanted to see me.

We arranged to meet up after lunch and I carried on clearing up the kitchen, thinking about the new show and how great it was that Phoebe had rung and how I couldn't wait for next Saturday.

I'd just about finished when I heard Mum come in.

"We're starting a new show at drama," I called out, rushing from the kitchen to meet her at the door. "Look! I've had a letter from Mandy and it sounds brilliant; it's all about computers and..."

The second I saw Mum's face I stopped. She was flushed and she looked weird, like she was excited about something but it was too secret to tell. She was holding the letter I'd signed for; clutching it to her chest like it was incredibly precious.

"What's the matter, Mum? Where have you been?"

She stared at me for the longest time. "Come and sit down, Polly," she said, finally. "I've got something to tell you."

2

Mum's News

"I'm just doing the dishes," I muttered, scooting back into the kitchen. I had no idea what Mum was going to say, but I could tell it was serious. "I've tidied up for you, look," I called out behind me.

Mum followed me in and pulled me away from the sink. "Never mind about that now, silly," she said. "I've got something really important to tell you. Come on, sit down here." She practically pushed me into a chair and sat down opposite. "I'm sorry about this morning, rushing off like that. I know I left the kitchen in a state but—"

"No, it's fine," I said, quickly. "It's great to see you all dressed up and busy and I've tidied everything away so don't worry. I was just going to tell you about drama and—"

"Polly, stop interrupting and just listen for a minute, will you?" Mum took my hands across the table and held them tight. "Now I know this is totally out of the blue, but the thing is, Pol..." She took a deep breath. "I've been offered a job."

"Well that's good, isn't it?" I said, even though I could tell it wasn't just by the way she was looking at me.

"Well, yes it *is* good, sweetheart. But you see it's not exactly a *local* job." She sort of laughed and then stopped suddenly.

"What do you mean? Where is it then?"

"Look, I don't want you getting yourself all upset, but the problem is it's not actually in *England*. It's...erm...quite far away you see...in Spain." Then she carried on, speaking really fast. "But it's only for a year, and it'll go in a flash. A year really isn't even that long when you think about it. I mean it's only twelve months. I actually found out yesterday when you were at your dad's – that's why the kitchen was in such a state, because Tracy and some of the girls came round to celebrate and..."

She went on and on about how she was going to be selling holiday homes to British tourists, and how she'd been on a course run by the company, and about how it was such a fantastic opportunity, but I stopped listening. I just sat there and watched her mouth move. *Spain!* My mum was taking me to *Spain*; taking me away from all my friends and from school and from drama. *Drama!* What about the new show? I was supposed to be meeting up with Phoebe. I was...

I pulled my hands away from her. "I'm not going!" I shouted. "I don't care what you say, you can't make me. It's not fair, I don't want to go to Spain. You can't just come home and say, *We're going to Spain.*" The last thing I wanted was to start over somewhere new where I didn't know anyone and I didn't even speak the stupid language.

"Calm down, Polly! You're not going to Spain, silly. You're not going anywhere, not really. Look, I haven't discussed it with your dad yet, but you know how I feel. I can't stay here right now, not with Diane parading the baby about every five minutes. You do understand, don't you, love?"

She pulled a tissue out of her pocket and started to dab at her eyes. I knew it had been awful for Mum since Dad left to live with Diane. How embarrassed she was about it all happening on the street, played out like some dreadful soap opera for all the neighbours to gawp at. But I still didn't get what she meant about *me* not going to Spain, about *me* not going anywhere really...and then I caught on.

"You think I'm going to live with Dad and Diane, don't you?" I leaped up. "You think you're going to swan off to Spain for a year and dump me with Dad and Diane and the baby. You don't care about me at all!"

I tore out the room and up the stairs.

"No one cares about me!" I screamed down to her, and then I burst out crying.

Mum came running after me and we sat on my bed talking for ages. She tried to explain how the break would be good for all of us, but I just didn't get it. If the choice was between going to Spain with Mum or moving in with Dad and Diane I know what I'd choose every time.

"But, Polly, you're always saying you want to see your dad more," Mum said, stroking my hair and trying not to cry. "I know you didn't mean you wanted to move in there exactly, but it will be great for you to spend some proper time with him – *and* with your new baby brother. And what about drama and all your friends? You love going to Star Makers.

You look forward to it all week."

I tried to take in what she was saying. Okay, maybe it would be good for her to get away – but not from *me*. And maybe it would be good to spend more time with Dad – but definitely *not* with Diane and Jake.

We were still going round in circles when Phoebe called back to say she couldn't come over after all. Her mum had popped out somewhere and she had to stay in with her little sister, Sara. She couldn't believe it when I told her what was going on.

"That's awful, Polly. I can see why you're upset. But at least your mum's not forcing you to go with her."

"Yeah I know, but I've got to find some way to make her stay. There must be *something* I can do."

"I'll help you think of something," she said, shyly. "Maybe we can find a way to make her change her mind together."

Sometimes I couldn't believe I'd been so mean to Phoebe last term *or* that she'd forgiven me. If someone had told me a few months back that we'd end up being friends I would've thought they were bonkers.

The rest of the week was a total nightmare. Mum called Dad first thing the next morning and basically told him I was moving in with them more or less straight away. Mum wasn't even leaving for another couple of weeks, but she said it would be best to get me settled at Dad's before term started. Couldn't wait to get rid of me more like. She didn't ask or anything, she just told him. After that there were endless phone calls, and Dad was on the doorstep shouting and carrying on. It was so obvious he didn't want me to live with them.

And in the meantime, Mum was packing up and saying goodbye to people and getting her nails done and coming home every day with bags of new clothes, as if she was going off on some two-week holiday, not disappearing out of my life for a whole year. She tried her best to hide how excited she was so I wouldn't get upset, but it was so obvious.

It turned out that the important letter – the one that had arrived that morning – was the actual contract she had to sign to accept the job. I tried everything to get her to change her mind. I promised I'd wash the dishes every day and make my bed and stop being so stroppy – but she just kept saying it was something she *had* to do and that one day when I was older I'd understand.

I spent most of the time lying on my bed cuddling Cosmo. I wasn't going anywhere without him – not even to Dad's. I'd had Cosmo since he was six weeks old and I couldn't bear to be separated from him.

"I'll never leave you," I whispered into his fur, and I wondered if maybe we should run away together. I tried to work out where we could go, but it was hopeless. Cats aren't like dogs. You can't just bundle them up and take them somewhere new.

Dad called me on my mobile a couple of times. Diane even called once and left some stupid message about how much Jakey was *looking forward to his big sister moving in*, as if it had all been their idea in the first place. I knew what Diane *really* thought of me – that I was moody and difficult and always in a sulk – so why on earth would she want someone like that to move in with her and her precious baby?

On Friday morning, Dad turned up to help me move. It was only seven houses away of course, but there was no way I could manage all the bags by myself. It's funny because Dad's actual job is helping people move house. He's got this massive white van and he's really strong and muscly from shifting so much heavy furniture. He calls himself **The Big Man with the Big Van** but this was probably the smallest job he'd ever done – shifting his own daughter seven houses up the road.

"All set?" he said, ruffling my hair. "We've got your room looking really nice. I know it's tiny but Diane's cleared out all the drawers and you've got your computer in there already. I reckon you'll be settled in no time."

"What about Cosmo?" I said. "I'm not going anywhere without Cosmo."

Cosmo had crawled under my bed and was refusing to come out. I was very tempted to crawl under there with him.

Dad put his head on one side and I could guess what was coming. "Well, you know Diane's never been too keen on cats, and she's a wee bit worried about Jakey. Let's get you moved in and sorted and then we can come back and get Cosmo tomorrow, or the day after, or next week some time. How does that sound?"

It didn't sound great, but I knew my opinion wasn't going to count for much so I just kept quiet. We trudged up and down the road, carrying my stuff bit by bit until my room at home was so empty it looked as if I'd never lived in it. Twelve whole years stuffed into a bunch of black bin liners. The only thing left when we'd finished was poor Cosmo, cowering and confused under my bed.

I only unpacked a few things at Dad's. Just enough to make it look like *my* room. I didn't want to get too settled because I wasn't planning on staying that long. I put my covers on the bed along with Boo, my tatty old beanie-bear that I'd had since I was tiny, and stuck a few photos up on the mirror.

I had planned to stay in my room all evening, but when Dad called me down for tea I suddenly realized how starving I was. The kitchen at Diane's is teeny and Dad looked so silly trying to lay the table and spoon food into Jake's mouth and sort out chopping the salad all at the same time.

"Here she is!" he announced as I walked in, as if I was some incredibly important visitor they'd all been dying to see.

The tea was awful and I'm not exaggerating. Diane had made this soggy spaghetti in a slimy, green sauce that looked like vomit – and then Jake actually puked up some of *his* tea, splattering bright orange carroty goo right down my new top.

"He couldn't help it, Polly," snapped Dad, as I screamed and sprang away from the table. "You were a baby once, you know. Now eat up and stop making such a fuss."

I pushed the spaghetti round my plate. It looked like a load of slithering, green worms and I wondered for a second if Diane was trying to poison me.

"I don't actually like green sauce," I muttered. I was very tempted to throw the whole lot straight into the bin, but I knew Dad would go off on one.

Diane laughed. "It's called pesto, Polly," she said. "It's Italian. Haven't you ever had it before? It's made from basil leaves."

"I don't care what sort of leaves it's made from. I'm not eating it, *all right*?"

Just then Jake squealed and banged his spoon and another lump of orange goo flew right into my face. Dad and Diane burst out laughing, clapping their hands as if he'd done something really clever.

"Oh, Polly, he's so excited to have you here," cried Diane. "You should be honoured!"

Back in my room I waited until everyone was asleep before I logged on to **THWACKERS**. I played for hours, improving my score each time, until by the time I logged off I'd moved up to second place on the leader board. At some point I heard Jake wake up because he'd lost his stupid dummy again. I heard Dad pleading with Diane to get up to sort him out and I heard her talking to him in her simpery,

soppy baby voice, but I just played on –
eliminating the bad guys as fast as they
appeared on the screen:

THWACK!

THWACK!

THWACK!

I was shattered the next morning. Diane fussed about me at breakfast, but the minute Jake started to howl from upstairs, she dashed out of the room and left me to get on by myself. I gulped down my cereal and raced off down the road to make sure Cosmo was okay.

He was waiting for me outside number 25. We sat on the doorstep and I told him all about the slimy, green spaghetti and how Diane was trying to poison me and how it wouldn't be long until we were back together again. He stared at me with his huge, tawny-coloured eyes and I swear he understood every word.

"Don't worry, Cosmo," I said, giving him the biggest cuddle. "I'll soon get Mum to change her mind about Spain and then I'll move back home and everything will go back to how it was before."

I didn't really believe that for a second, but I couldn't bear to see him so sad.

Dad drove me up to drama in his van. You have to climb up really high to get into the front and when I was younger we used to play this stupid game that Dad was the King and I was his precious Princess Polly and we'd drive around looking down on everyone in our kingdom, checking that everything was in order. "Where to, Princess Polly?" he'd say in this silly posh voice. "Your wish is my command."

We didn't say much on the way to drama today – well, I didn't anyway. Dad went on and on about how well I was settling in and how I was still his *Princess Polly*, but I just stared out of the window trying to work out how I was going to stop Mum from going away. As soon as we arrived, I scrambled down from the van and disappeared inside.

It was strange walking back into drama and seeing everyone after the break – especially as so much had changed since last term. Phoebe was over by the piano with Ellie, Sam and Monty B. Ellie used to be Phoebe's best friend – they'd been friends since nursery – but when they started Woodville Secondary, Ellie became best friends with Sam, and Phoebe was left tagging along after them.

Now Phoebe and I were starting to get close and I could just imagine us being really good friends – if it wasn't for the *Great* Montgomery Brown – also known as the *Not*-So-Great Monty B. He was Phoebe's next-door neighbour years and years ago and, basically, he's got the BIGGEST crush on her. She swears blind he hasn't, but it's so obvious.

They were all laughing their heads off about something, but as soon as Phoebe spotted me she came straight over and gave me a quick hug.

"Let's go over to the others," she said, pulling me back towards them, but I shook my head. I still felt weird around Phoebe's friends after last term when I was so mean to her. She might have forgotten about it, but there's no way they had – especially Monty B. And anyway, I was dying to tell her about Diane and the green spaghetti.

I was just about to launch into the whole story when Mandy called us over to sit in a circle. Her hair was a little bit longer than before the holidays and a perfectly ordinary brown colour.

"Hi, guys," she said, grinning. "It's so great to see you all. I really missed you over the holidays, believe it or not!"

I looked around the circle at all the old faces and a couple of new ones I didn't recognize.

"What's happened to your hair, Mandy?"

said Monty B. "I'm sure last time we saw you it was a sort of psychedelic shade of purple."

She pulled a face. "I'm not allowed to dye it for a bit, worse luck. The hairdresser said it was in such a shocking state it was in danger of falling out at any minute!"

Monty B ran his hand through his bright red hair. "I was going to stop dying mine as well," he said, "but Phoebe literally begged me not to."

"No I didn't!" Phoebe cried, slapping him. "You can shave it right off for all I care!"

"Okay, okay, enough about hair," said Mandy. "I actually spent most of the break working on our new production, CRASH! It's a fantastic adventure story all about how dangerous computers can be."

"Have you got the scripts with you today?" Sam called out. "I hope there are loads of big parts!"

"I have but, before we get started, I want to

welcome Sandeep and Rachel, who've joined Star Makers today."

Phoebe squeezed my hand. "It's so nice not being new this term, isn't it?" she whispered. I nodded, smiling. It was nice not being new but it was even nicer being friends with Phoebe.

"We're going to go round the circle and say our names and three facts about ourselves. Your favourite colour, something you did in the holidays, anything. I'll go first, and then we'll carry on round to the right."

The new girl looked a bit worried.

"Don't worry, Rachel," said Mandy, noticing straight away. "You can just say your name if you prefer. Okay, let's start. I'm Mandy. My favourite film is *The Wizard of Oz*. I love banana and Marmite sandwiches and my middle name is George, because my parents were secretly hoping I'd be a boy."

"Have I ever told you what *my* middle name is?" said Monty B.

"Oh my God, yeah, it's not Bumble, is it?" said one of the older girls, Neesha. "You know, as in, Monty Bumble **B**!"

"No it's not actually," said Monty B. "My parents aren't *that* stupid!"

Catharine went next. She's in Year Nine and she had the main part in our first show last term. "I've got two sisters," she said. "I'm allergic to pink marshmallows and I raised forty-five pounds in the holiday, doing a charity swim."

Rachel said her name and smiled. She was really pretty with rosy cheeks and dimples and I don't know why, but she annoyed me straight away – flashing her dimples at everyone like that.

Monty B was sitting next to Rachel. "My name's Monty B," he said. "I'm not allergic to pink marshmallows but I *am* seriously allergic to pink. I can't even be in the same room as something pink without feeling sick. It's ever since I had to wear that tutu in the last show. The awful thing is, my nan's knitting me these pink socks for my birthday and I don't know how to tell her that I won't be able to wear them. It's terrible really because—"

"I said FACTS," said Mandy, laughing. "Not a load of made-up nonsense."

"But it's all true," insisted Monty B. "That tutu has scarred me for life."

"Ah bless," said Neesha. "It's just *tu tu* sad."

"You will not believe this, Mandy," said Ellie, when it got to her turn. "But I actually *lost* my brother during the holidays."

"That doesn't surprise me in the slightest, Ellie Matthews," said Mandy, shaking her head. "A week doesn't go by without you losing something. I presume you found him again."

"I did, and luckily it was before my mum and dad realized he was lost. Oh, I'm Ellie by the way," she said, smiling round at Sandeep and Rachel.

Sandeep was really cool-looking, with his long, shiny black hair tied back in a pony tail.

"I'm Sandeep and I'm in Year Nine," he said. "I *love* acting, but I've never done any singing or dancing, so I'll probably make a total idiot of myself."

"Don't worry," I said. "We've got Monty B for that."

"Very funny," said Monty B, but Sandeep burst out laughing and winked at me.

I didn't have a clue what to say when it got to my turn. I wasn't about to tell everyone that my mum was leaving me to go and live in Spain and that I'd been forced to live with my dad and his wicked girlfriend. The last thing I wanted was for everyone to feel sorry for me, but I couldn't think of anything else. I sat there looking down at my lap.

"Shall we come back to you, Polly?" said Mandy. "Give you a bit more time?"

"No, it's okay," I said. I took a deep breath and looked up. Sandeep winked at me again and Rachel flashed her dimples. "My name's Polly," I said, as if I didn't have a care in the world. "I've got an amazing cat called Cosmo who understands everything I say to him. My mum's going to work in Spain but it's brilliant because I'm going to visit her there on holiday *all the time* and I've got a new brother called Jake who's easily the most gorgeous baby in the world."

Phoebe gave me a funny look, but I turned to face the other way.

When we'd gone all the way round the circle we did the rapping name-game and then we did some other games in groups. I stayed as far away from Phoebe as I could – I didn't want her to start asking me about what I'd said. She paired up with Rachel and they seemed to be having a great time together, laughing and mucking around. I nearly went over to see what the big joke was, but just then Mandy called us back to the circle to tell us more about CRASH!

"Basically, it's about this sad and very lonely girl called Marcia Moon. She's in her room playing her favourite game on her computer when she accidentally types in a secret code, and from that moment on things start to go very wrong."

"But why is the main character always a girl?" complained Monty B. "Can't she be called Marc instead of Marcia?"

"Well, technically speaking I suppose she could," said Mandy. "But Marcia's not the only good part. There are the viruses – led by the most lethal virus of all, Cydore. And then there's Tarn – the boy who's been trapped inside the computer game for years – and heaps more. I'll hand the scripts out after break and we'll have a read-through."

"What did you say all that stuff for?" said

Phoebe, as we walked to the back of the hall with our bags. "You know, about your mum leaving and about Jake? I thought you said you couldn't stand him."

"Listen, I haven't told you about Diane trying to poison me last night," I said, changing the subject.

"*Poison you?*" said Phoebe. "What do you mean?"

I told her all about the green slime, and how Diane was trying to be really nice to cover up how she really felt about me moving in.

"You never know," said Phoebe, shrugging. "I mean, maybe she's okay about you being there?"

"*What?*" I stared at her. "*No way!* You don't know what you're talking about."

"*Okay*, I'm just saying."

Just then Monty B came over to sit with us.

"Come on then," said Phoebe. "What's your middle name?"

"It's top secret, I'm afraid. If I tell you, I'll have to kill you."

"Go on. Just tell me the first letter."

"No, Phoebs! I mean it, I'm not saying."

"You're lucky he's even sitting with you," said Adam, coming over with Sam and Ellie. "I mean, you are wearing a pink top, Phoebe." Adam's in Year Nine and he's really cute. Sam and Ellie were both crazy about him last term, giggling like idiots every time he even spoke to them, but I had a funny feeling Sandeep was going to be the latest Star Makers' heart-throb.

"I was joking about the pink thing," said Monty B. "I loved wearing that tutu, didn't I, Phoebs?"

"How should I know?" said Phoebe, giggling.

"Because you know *everything* about me."

Phoebe shook her finger at him. "Except your middle name," she said.

I sat there watching them muck about. I could've joined in, I suppose, but I didn't want to. Now that Phoebe and I were friends, I couldn't help feeling a bit jealous of Monty B and the others. I wanted to talk to her about Cosmo, and my mum leaving and stuff, but I knew I'd never get her to myself – not with everyone else hanging around.

"The show sounds amazing, doesn't it?" said Sam. "I really, *really* want to be Marcia – not that I'd ever be stupid enough to give out my personal details on the computer."

"It's going to be Marc, not Marcia," said Monty B. "So bad luck, Sam."

I wasn't that bothered if it was Marc or Marcia. I wasn't that bothered about the show full stop. All I could think about was Mum leaving for Spain and me trapped for a whole year at Dad and Diane's. I mean, it's not like Mum would even be here to see me perform, so what was the point?

And then, suddenly, a little thought popped into my head – and the minute it was in there it started to grow BIGGER and BIGGER. It was so obvious I couldn't believe I hadn't thought of it sooner. Mum was always going on about how much she loved the last show and how she couldn't wait to see me up on the stage again. So maybe the only way to stop her going to Spain – the *one* thing that might make her rethink the whole stupid plan – was for ME to get the starring role in CRASH!

Marc or Marcia?

As soon as break was over and we were sitting back in a circle, I asked Mandy if I could be Marcia when we read through the script. I knew the auditions wouldn't be for at least a week but I wanted her to know straight away that I was interested in getting a big part: that I *had* to get a big part to stop Mum going away.

"Sorry, Polly, but like I said, it's going to be *Marc*, not Marcia," said Monty B.

"No, it isn't," I snapped. "Why should you decide anyway? Mandy wrote it as Marcia, so it's Marcia."

"Listen, Polly," said Mandy. "I know I wrote it as Marcia, but Monty B does have a point. I'll have a think about it and I'll let you know next week. And yes, Polly, you can read Marcia's part in Act One – and then someone else can have a go in Act Two."

Sam's hand shot up and she started bleating on about how desperate *she* was to be Marcia. I had a quick look round at some of the other girls. I was pretty certain Catharine wouldn't get a main part this time, because she'd had the biggest part in the last show. Ellie didn't really want a big part, neither did Neesha, and I wasn't sure if Phoebe would be confident enough. But Sam was the most confident person I'd ever met in my life *and* she had a really good singing voice.

"Okay, Sam," said Mandy, handing round the scripts. "You can read Marcia's part in Act Two. But it's just a read-through, girls, not an audition."

Sam glanced over at me and I knew what she was thinking. I stared her down. She wasn't the only one who was desperate to get the main part and I could be pretty determined when I set my mind to it.

The show opens with Marcia sitting alone at her computer. She's playing her favourite game, The Rainbow Room, when she accidentally types in a secret code and the computer starts talking to her. She's really excited at first, because she thinks if she talks back she might improve her score. But as the scene goes on, the computer threatens her and demands all sorts of personal information, and she ends up totally freaked out.

She tries to log off but it's too late and at the end of the scene she gets sucked right through the screen and into the game. Once she's in there, the only way she can escape is to work out the new code – but if she fails to crack the code before her computer crashes, she'll be trapped for ever.

We started reading through and I tried to sound as frightened as I could. I tried to think of all the scary things that could happen to me, like finding a massive spider in my bed, or getting lost in the middle of the night, and it wasn't that difficult really. I *was* frightened. Frightened Mum would fly off to Spain and leave me stuck at Dad's for a whole year with Desperate Di and The Great Baby Jake.

"That was fantastic, Polly!" said Mandy, when we got to the end of the first scene. "Let's stop for a minute and I'll play you the opening number. You'll love it!"

Phoebe linked arms with me as we walked across the hall over to the piano. "You were brilliant, Polly. You sounded absolutely terrified."

"Yeah but you haven't heard *me* yet," said Sam, pushing past us.

"I don't even know if I'll be brave enough to audition," said Phoebe. "Remember what happened last term? I was too scared to try."

"Yes, but Phoebe, you did end up singing

that solo at the end of the show and it was wicked."

"No it wasn't!" she said. Her face turned so red her freckles practically disappeared, but I could tell she was pleased.

We stood around the piano while Mandy talked us through the opening song.

"The first song starts while the computer is talking to Marcia. It's called 'Give Me Your Name – Give Me Your Number', and basically it's the computer bullying Marcia until she feels she has no choice but to do whatever it wants."

"You know, it's actually very dangerous to give out your personal details on the computer," said Tara Perkins, peering through her little round glasses. "There was something in the news last week about a girl our age who'd gone on this site called friend2friend – it's a chatroom or something – and she got into all sorts of trouble."

I'd heard about friend2friend – it was one of the websites Dad had forbidden me from going on when he bought my laptop.

"Yes, well that's the whole point of the show, Tara," said Mandy. "But I'm sure none of you would ever be silly enough to give out your personal details to anyone."

"Oh my God, yeah," said Neesha, rolling her eyes. "My parents practically sit on my lap while *I'm* using the computer. I couldn't do anything stupid like Marcia, even if I wanted to."

"It's *Marc* not Marcia," said Monty B, but no one took any notice.

Mandy handed out the words and played through the music a couple of times.

"Everyone, apart from Marcia, is going to sing the chorus as the computer," she explained, "while Marcia shouts, *No!* and *Get out of my head!* and *Leave me alone!* I'll sing Marcia's part for now until we know who's going to play her."

The chorus was quite tricky. The timing had to be just right, so we went over and over each line until eventually we were ready to put it all together.

"Okay, let's take it from the top," said Mandy, playing the introduction. "And try to sound as sinister as you can."

We all sang a bit hesitantly at first, but by the final chorus we were belting it out.

Give me your name – give me your number,
Now is the time to understand the rules,
That I am the one with the tools,
To teach you, to reach you, to show you
That I am the master and you must obey the rules!
Yes, I am the master and you must obey the rules!
Give me your name – give me your number,
Give me your number, yeah, give it to me!
Give me your number, then you will see!
Give me your number, I'll count to three!

Give me your number – give it to me…

One…two…

We'd just about got to the end when the door flew open and Arthur burst in. Arthur's the man who rents Mandy the hall and he looks pretty sinister himself. He wears this weird, black cloak and he's got a manky beard that's always full of leftover food.

"Hello, Mandy!" he boomed, striding over to the piano.

"Oh, hello, Arthur," said Mandy, in a really cheery voice. We looked at her, surprised.

"Why's she being so friendly?" hissed Phoebe. "The last time she saw him she was ready to kill him."

"Beats me." I shrugged.

"What a pleasure to have you back after the holidays," said Arthur. "And what theatrical masterpiece are you conjuring up for us this time?"

"It's called CRASH!" said Mandy, still

grinning from ear to ear. If she grinned any harder her face would split open. "It's about a girl who gets trapped inside a computer."

"Or boy," said Monty B.

"Oh marvellous," said Arthur. "I've just got a new computer myself but I haven't the faintest idea what it's supposed to do. I leave all that to Mrs. Beagle on the church funding committee. She's simply a whiz at all this modern technology."

Mandy's face didn't change. Not even at the mention of Mrs. Beagle, who'd sold all our costumes at a church jumble sale last term – two weeks before the show!

"Was it anything in particular, Arthur?" she said, still beaming. "Only we're just learning the opening number."

"Carry on, carry on," said Arthur. He put his hands together and bowed. "I'll leave you to your creativity. Just one thing," he said, stopping at the door. "I'm organizing a ballroom dance event to raise some money for charity. There'll be a panel of judges and the winners will receive a sumptuous summer picnic hamper."

Phoebe squeezed my hand and I tried not to laugh.

"Tickets are in my office if anyone would like to support the cause," Arthur went on, tugging at his beard. "All the money raised will go towards buying a piano for the old people's home in Cranbourne. I'm actually taking part myself, so while I'd love to stay and chat, I really should be off to practise my foxtrot!"

And with that, he disappeared, his cloak billowing out behind him.

"Are you okay, Mandy?" asked Monty B.

"I'm fine," said Mandy, but she wasn't smiling any more. She slumped down onto the piano stool as if the effort of being nice to Arthur had worn her out. "It's just that I decided during the holidays that I wasn't going to let Arthur get to me any more. I know he means well, but it was one thing after the other last term. I really can't cope with any more lost costumes or fish on the walls. This term I'm just going to smile and pretend he doesn't really exist – not in any meaningful way that could affect my life."

"Is it working?" asked Catharine.

"Erm...ask me in a few weeks," said Mandy.

"But what do you mean exactly by *fish on the walls*?" asked Sandeep.

"Trust me," said Catharine. "You really don't want to know!"

We carried on singing for a bit. Mandy put Sandeep with the altos, because his voice was really low and deep, and Rachel with the sopranos. I was itching to try out Marcia's part, just to see if I could do it, but I knew I'd have to wait.

When we'd finished Sam had her turn reading Marcia's part and, I hate to admit it, but she was really good. Monty B had a quick go too, being Marc, but he kept adding bits and he refused to give the computer his name and code, which would obviously change the whole story.

"I'm not taking this seriously, you know," said Mandy, trying to keep a straight face.

Neesha rolled her eyes. "Oh my God, yeah, I'd be worried if you did start taking him seriously," she said. "You do know his middle name is Moron!"

"No it's not!" said Monty B. "It's—"

But he stopped himself just in time, clapping his hand over his mouth.

We ended the session with my favourite game, SPLAT! I was splatting people so fast it was like playing **THWACKERS** on the computer: Splat! Splat! Splat! Until the only two people left were me and Sam.

"Oh look, we've run out of time," said Mandy, glancing up at the clock. "Never mind, we'll

have two winners today. Well done, you guys."
Everyone cheered and it was a great way to
end the session, but I knew that when it came
to casting the show there was only room for
one winner and it wasn't going to be Sam Lester
– not if I had anything to do with it.

"There's just one thing I'd like you to do at
home," said Mandy before we left. "Pick a
scene – any scene you like as long as it's only
got two characters. Practise until you can
perform it without using a script and then we'll
pair up and take a look at them next
Saturday."

"Do you mean like an audition?" asked Sam.

"Yes, I suppose it will be an audition in
a way," said Mandy. "We're going to be
performing the show in June, so we've really
got to get going."

Mum was waiting for me downstairs. She'd
decided that we should spend the rest of the
day together, shopping. It was supposed to

cheer me up or something. We set off up to the chemist so she could buy some suncream and other bits for Spain. She spent ages walking round the aisles picking up all sorts of lotions and potions until her basket was practically overflowing.

At the make-up counter we both tried on some new lipstick, squashing together to see our faces in the tiny, cracked mirror. Mum chose the brightest red she could find and then kissed my cheek hard, giggling like a teenager.

"How was drama?" she asked, kissing me again and again until my cheek was covered in crimson kiss marks. "I bet it was nice to see everyone?"

I couldn't remember the last time I'd seen her this happy. I was dying to tell her about the show and about how much I wanted to be Marcia, but I decided to keep quiet. It would be so much more exciting to tell her when the part was mine.

5
Beanie-bear,
Boo, to the Rescue

I didn't mind being at Dad and Diane's so much now that I had a plan. Instead of playing **THWACKERS** that night, I read right through CRASH! and chose a scene for my audition. I wanted to do something really dramatic to try and convince Mandy I was the right person for the part. The best scene was in Act Two, when Marcia meets Tarn for the first time inside the computer.

Marcia's running down the inside of an electric cable trying to get away from Cydore, the deadliest of all the viruses, when Tarn appears suddenly and helps her escape. Tarn tells Marcia that he's been trying to crack the secret code for years and that real time stands

still when you're inside the game.

Tarn: That's why I'm still thirteen. I've been trapped for so long but when I get out my parents won't even know I've been missing.

Marcia: My parents wouldn't notice if I went missing anyway. They don't notice I'm alive half the time. Sometimes I wonder why they bothered to have me in the first place.

Tarn: But that's why you're here, Marcia. They search for the kids who don't have anyone to look out for them.

Marcia: What do you mean, *That's the reason I'm here*? And who are *they*? You're scaring me, Tarn.

Tarn: You'll find out soon enough…come on, someone's coming and it might be Cydore. Follow me!

They make a pact to look out for each other and, even though Marcia is trapped, she

actually feels less lonely stuck in the computer with Tarn than she does in her real life.

When Dad came in to say goodnight he offered to read Tarn's part, so I could practise properly, but I shook my head. "No thanks."

"Come on, Princess Polly. It might help you with the audition."

"What do you care? Anyway, I'm *not* your princess and I don't need any help. Not from you."

Dad sighed and walked over to the door. I could see he was upset, but that was his problem. He stopped in the doorway and turned to look at me.

"You know, I was in a play once at school," he said. "I had to kiss this girl, Kelly Bates, but it was a nightmare. She kept making this really stupid face, screwing up her eyes and sticking her head forward, as if kissing me was the worst thing in the world. There was no way I could do it. I nearly burst trying not to laugh every time I even looked at her.

"'For pity's sake, Simon – just kiss her!' Mrs. Mulbury, the drama teacher would shout, but I couldn't. For years after that all my mates used to tease me about it. 'For pity's sake, Simon, just kiss her!' they'd shout out whenever a girl walked past us – *any* girl. It put me off acting for life!"

He looked over at me with his head on the side, practically pleading with me to say something. I tried to imagine him on the stage with Kelly Bates, trying not to laugh, and I nearly smiled – but I forced myself not to.

"Well, give me a shout if you change your mind. I don't mind acting again if it's to help my princess."

He hung around by the door for ages, as if I was going to change my mind that second.

"Can you close the door behind you?" I said in the end. The longer he stood there the closer I came to saying sorry, or throwing myself into his arms for a cuddle, and there was no way I was going to do that.

In the morning, I didn't even hang about to eat breakfast. I raced straight off to see Cosmo. If my plan worked, and I got Mum to change her mind about Spain, it would only be another couple of weeks until I could move back in.

"You'd best stay here in the meantime," I said, cuddling him on the doorstep. "There's no point putting you through all that upheaval for such a short amount of time, is there – you'll only end up confused."

He pushed his face right into mine, over and over.

"I miss you too, Cosmo," I said, sighing. "But the auditions are on Saturday so we should find out our parts before Mum's due to leave. I reckon we're talking two weeks tops."

We cuddled for a bit longer and then I went inside to see Mum. She was in the kitchen listening to her Learn Spanish in a Month CD.

"*Hola, Polly!*" she cried as I came in. "*Buenos dias.*"

"Can I have some breakfast?" I said. I put a slice of bread in the toaster.

"That means, 'Hello, Polly, good morning.' What do you think of my accent?" She pulled a face and groaned. "I know, I know, it's dreadful. No one's going to understand a word I say. How about this then? *Cómo te llamas?*"

"Is there any peanut butter?" I rummaged through the cupboard. "Why is there *never* anything to eat in this house any more?"

"Come on, Polly. *Cómo te llamas?* That means, 'What is your name?' You have to say, *Me llamo Polly.* Repeat it after me."

"You already know my name and anyway *I'm* not going to Spain so *I* don't need to learn Spanish. Why don't *you* repeat *that* after *me*!" I pressed stop on the CD player and put on some really loud music.

Mum turned it off and sat me down at the table.

"Don't be like that, Pol. I know how upsetting this is for you and I'm going to miss you like mad, but it won't be as bad as you think."

"You keep saying that, but it's not you who has to live at Dad's with Desperate Di and The Great Baby Jake."

Mum's eyes filled with tears and I was sorry as soon as the words were out of my mouth.

"More like *Desperate Me*, dumped on my own doorstep," she sniffed.

"You're not desperate!" I cried. "It shouldn't be you running away from the street. It's so unfair."

It went on like that for the rest of the week. Dad trying to be my best friend and Mum twittering on about her accent and her Spanish phrases one minute and collapsing in tears the next.

"They're driving me insane," I said to Phoebe

on Wednesday at school. "You should have heard Dad at breakfast this morning, talking to me as if I was one of his mates, asking me for advice about this removals job he's got on. He never used to talk to me about stuff like that before I moved in there."

"I don't know why you're complaining. My dad's so busy he doesn't even notice I'm there half the time."

"This is different," I muttered. "Anyway, have you chosen a scene yet? For the auditions?"

Phoebe took her script out of her school bag.

"I'm going to do this one from Act Two," she said, showing me. "It's when Marcia meets the main character from the computer game. Her name's Rainbow, remember? I'll read it through now if you want. I could really do with the practice."

We walked over to a corner of the

playground so no one else could hear. She didn't sound very confident and I could tell she was worried.

"Do you actually want to be Marcia?" I asked when she'd finished.

"I'm not bothered really – I just want a big singing part. You know how much I love singing. How about you?"

"I'm not bothered either," I said. I felt bad about lying to Phoebe but I was too scared to tell her how desperate I was to be Marcia, just in case the whole plan went wrong.

We practised for a bit longer until Ellie and Sam came over to see what we were doing. Sam grabbed hold of Phoebe's script and clutched it to her chest.

"I can't *wait* for Saturday," she said, dramatically. "I bet you anything I'm going to be Marcia and Adam's going to be Tarn." She was so sure of herself it was as if she could see straight into the future. "Or maybe the new boy, Sandeep, will be Tarn. Did you see the way he kept winking at me last week?"

"Make your mind up," said Ellie. "I thought it was Adam you fancied! And anyway, he was winking at everyone. He probably had something in his eye."

We all burst out laughing and Ellie started to wink at Sam.

"Oh, Sam, you're so beautiful," she crooned, winking and blinking like mad. "Your silky hair, your gorgeous curvy figure, your...erm... healthy, pink gums!"

"*What!*" spluttered Phoebe, laughing so much I thought she was going to choke. "*Healthy pink gums?*"

"I ran out of things to say," said Ellie, shrugging her shoulders and grinning. "Anyway I bet *some* boys notice how healthy your gums are. That's what my mum always says when she's nagging me to brush my teeth!"

* * *

Later that afternoon, I was upstairs at Dad's practising my scene when Jake started to howl. I tried to carry on but the crying got louder and louder and even with my door closed it was as if he was screaming right into my ear. It went on and on and I was just about to storm downstairs when Diane burst into my room clutching hold of Jake in one hand and a manky, old tea towel in the other.

"Give me a hand, would you, Polly?" she shouted over Jake. "He's in a right state and I'm trying to get his tea cooked." She was in a state as well. Her top was covered in milky stains and she looked as if she was about to burst into tears.

"I'm in the middle of practising something for drama," I said. "I'll come and help in a bit."

"I'll just pop him down here then," she said, totally ignoring me. "There you go, sweetheart." She lay him down on the rug next to my bed. "It's his teeth," she went on. "He's got a big one coming through at the back and it must be killing him. I'll call up when his tea's ready."

Jake carried on screaming through all of this, banging his little fists on the rug and rolling from side to side.

"Thanks," said Diane, and she disappeared back downstairs.

I tried to carry on learning my scene but it was impossible. If I thought the screaming was loud when it was coming from downstairs, it was totally deafening right there in my tiny room.

"Come on, Jake," I muttered. "It can't hurt that much, can it? It's only a tooth!"

I glanced around for something to distract him. I'd never looked after a baby before – it had always been just me and Mum and Dad at home. The only thing lying about was Boo, my old beanie-bear. I picked him up and held him just above Jake's head, wiggling and waggling Boo about to try and get his attention.

For a minute, Jake just carried on wailing, his eyes closed and his fists curled up tight, but then, as he stopped to draw breath, he opened his eyes just a fraction and one of his tiny hands reached up for Boo. I lifted Boo a bit higher and carried on wiggling and he opened his eyes wider and reached up with both hands.

After a bit I stopped wiggling and he looked at me with a slightly puzzled expression on his face. I thought he might start crying again, so I wiggled Boo some more and Jake started to pump his podgy legs in and out, making little squealy noises like a mouse. Every time I stopped wiggling he stopped pumping and fixed me with his huge green eyes. So I wiggled again and he pumped again and after three or four more times, he started to giggle.

I was so busy wiggling I didn't hear Diane come back up. "Tea's ready," she said, coming in the room. She stopped at the door and stared.

"Polly, you're a star! Look at him giggling away!"

She picked up Jake, who immediately struggled to get down. He reached across her for Boo, his bottom lip starting to wobble. "Oh, can I bring your beanie-bear down, do you mind?" said Diane. "Just to keep him happy while he's eating."

I shrugged and handed him over. Jake clutched Boo to his chest and started to suck on his ear. I nearly grabbed him back, but I couldn't stand the thought of the screaming starting up all over again. That night I walked past Dad and Diane's room where Jake was sleeping in his cot. He was lying on his back holding on to Boo for dear life, sucking away at his mangled ear – just like I used to when I was a baby.

What Would Scooby Doo?

I practised and practised my scene until I knew it off by heart. I didn't want to leave anything to chance. Every time Jake started screaming or Dad tried to be my best mate, or Diane did her big *sucking up* act, it made me even more determined to do the best audition of my life. I felt awful about Cosmo as well, sitting on the wall outside number 25, waiting for me to appear at the top of the road. I kept telling him it was only for another week or so but I swear his eyes grew sadder with each passing day.

I couldn't wait to get to drama on Saturday. I *was* nervous about the auditions, but only because there was so much at stake. If I messed up, Sam would probably get the part of

Marcia and then I'd *never* get Mum to stay in England.

We played a few warm-up games to start off with and then Mandy sat us down in a circle.

"I've made a list of pairs," she said, taking a file out of her bag. "So in a minute, when you know who you're with, I want you to decide between you whose scene you're going to perform first – and then after break you can swap round and the other person will get to do theirs."

"Oh, Mandy, you'll never believe what happened!" cried Ellie.

Mandy rolled her eyes. "Let me guess. You lost your script, so you haven't been able to learn a scene for the auditions?"

"Well I didn't lose my *script* exactly," said Ellie. "I lost my *bag* and my script just happened to be *in* my bag. Luckily, my bag was found, you see I left it on the bus, but—"

"Wait!" Mandy held up her hand. "Don't

tell me. The script wasn't in there."

"How on earth did you know?" said Ellie, amazed. But Mandy just shook her head, sighing, and started to read out the pairs.

"Okay, I want Tara to go with Neesha. Ellie can pair up with Phoebe, Sam with Sandeep, Catharine with Adam, Polly with Monty B and—"

"Hang on a minute!" I burst out. "I can't be partners with Monty B!"

I couldn't do my audition with Monty B, the most stupid person in the whole, entire group!

I looked at Mandy in horror but she carried on reading out the list as if I hadn't said a word and everything was fine.

"Can I swap with you?" I begged Phoebe. "*Please.* You go with Monty B and I'll go with Ellie."

"Erm, well *I* don't mind," said Phoebe. "Just check with Mandy first."

But Mandy wasn't interested. "Come on,

Polly," she said. "Don't make a big deal out of this. You have to be able to get on with everyone when you're part of a group."

"But Monty B will just mess about," I said. "You know he will. He'll do something really stupid and ruin my chance of getting a good part."

"No I won't," said Monty B. "I'm not that thrilled about being with you either, if you must know. And anyway why would I mess about when I've got my heart set on being Marc?"

"*It's not Marc!*" I hissed. "*It's Marcia.*"

"Okay, calm down," he said, as if *I* was the one with the problem.

"I'm sorry but I can't be with him." I shook my head. "Seriously, Mandy, I'm not going to audition." My hands were itching to hit him. "I even don't care about getting a good part any more."

"I know you don't mean that, Polly," said Mandy. "Remember how well you read Marcia's part last week? I was really looking forward to watching you audition today."

I looked over at Monty B. He was grinning like an idiot and I knew he'd do something moronic, but then I thought of Mum getting ready to fly off to Spain, and Cosmo sitting on the wall outside number 25, waiting for me, and I knew I had to try.

"Okay," I muttered. "I'll do it."

"Right, off you go with your partners for a practice and we'll start in about twenty minutes."

"I'm with Sandeep," boasted Sam, as she swept past us, as if Sandeep had personally chosen her to be his partner. Sandeep glanced at us over Sam's head and winked. I remembered Ellie messing about at school, winking and blinking, but it didn't seem nearly so funny now that Sam was paired up with Sandeep for the auditions and I was stuck with Monty B.

"What scene have you chosen then?" he said, when we'd found a place to practise at the back of the hall.

"The one where Marcia meets Tarn for the first time – you know, when she's running away from Cydore."

"You're kidding! Me too."

"Well we can't both read Marcia's part, so you might as well be Tarn."

"Fine by me. The second I read Tarn's part at home I knew Mandy had written it with me in mind. It was so obvious."

I didn't mention that a minute ago he'd said he wanted to be Marc. I didn't really care if it meant I could be Marcia. "Just don't mess about, okay? It's a really dramatic scene. There are no funny bits in it at all."

"Stop stressing, Polly! I can do serious, right?"

I looked at him standing there with his dyed-red hair sticking out in a million different directions, wearing a T-shirt with **"What would Scooby Doo?"** written across the front, and I knew he'd never been serious in his whole, entire life.

We read through the scene a couple of times and I hate to admit it, but he was quite good. The problem was I knew he'd never be able to keep it up – not when the others were watching.

"Let's try and do it without scripts," I suggested after a bit. "But don't change the words or anything."

It sounds crazy, I know, but I actually began to enjoy myself. It was better than practising on my own at Dad's and I loved the script so much – especially Marcia's part. We did it once more and Mandy came over to watch us.

"Hey, you two are great," she said, and scribbled something in her file.

"See," said Monty B. "It's not so bad being partners with me after all, is it?"

"We haven't done it in front of everyone else yet. I know what happens to you every time you get anywhere near a stage, especially when you've got an audience."

Monty B shook his head. "You know what your problem is?" he said. "You need to learn how to trust me."

"As if," I said, but I couldn't help smiling.

We had just enough time to run it once more before Mandy called us over and the auditions began. Sam and Sandeep were first up and they were brilliant. Sam's just got this way of strutting about the stage as if she's the only person in the world who could possibly play the part.

Catharine and Adam were really good as well, but I was pretty sure Mandy wouldn't give Catharine the biggest part again. Ellie giggled all the way through her scene with Phoebe. She had to use a script and she kept losing her place. It's a shame Mandy didn't pair her up with Monty B – they would've made the perfect couple.

"Don't stress, Polly," he said, while we were waiting for our turn. "We'll wipe the floor with them."

I looked at him. "Do you swear you're not going to change any of the lines, or say something stupid, or start leaping around the stage?"

"I swear," he said. "Cross my beating heart."

"Polly and Monty B," Mandy called out, and suddenly I felt horribly nervous. This was my Big Chance, but what if I wasn't as good as Sam? What if Mandy had no intention of giving me a main part? What if she'd already decided who she wanted to cast as Marcia? What if... But then I stopped and somehow managed to shove all the negative thoughts out of my head. I marched onto the stage as if I didn't have a care in the world. I had to do a good audition

– there was so much at stake. I wasn't about to let a stupid bout of nerves ruin everything.

The scene went really well. It was amazing. I totally forgot I was on the stage with Monty B; he was Tarn and I was Marcia and we were trapped and frightened and the evil virus, Cydore, was after us. I knew we were good. There wasn't a sound in the hall and Mandy didn't take her eyes off us for a second.

I grabbed Monty B's arm looking round for Cydore. "What are we going to do?" I cried. "I'm so frightened, Tarn! I want to go home."

Monty B looked at me. He was supposed to say, "We're going to crack the code together and get out of here." It was the final line in the scene and I couldn't believe how well it was going. Just one last line and it would be over. I could almost hear Mandy telling me the part was mine.

"What are we going to do?" I said again, just in case Monty B had forgotten his line. I nudged him with my foot. But he just stared at me and suddenly I knew he was going to say something stupid. It was like an illness. He couldn't help himself.

"What are we going to do?" said Monty B. "I'm not sure, Marcia. But the real question is, what would *Scooby* Doo?" He pointed at his T-shirt, nodding at me like an idiot.

I opened my mouth but nothing came out.

"I said, what would *Scooby* Doo?" Monty B repeated, and the whole group collapsed laughing, including Mandy, as he started to dance around the stage singing the Scooby Doo theme tune at the top of his voice.

"You're such a moron!" I yelled. "Why do you always have to ruin everything?" I stormed off the stage and out of the hall.

I sat by myself in the break. I was so furious with Monty B *and* with everyone else for laughing. Phoebe kept trying to get me to come and sit with them but I didn't want to.

"Oh, just leave her alone," Sam called out in the end. "She's in a big sulk over nothing."

Phoebe shrugged helplessly. "Come on, Polly," she said. "The other day you said you weren't all that bothered about being Marcia."

"Yeah, well, that was the other day," I muttered. It wasn't her fault. She just didn't realize how important the auditions were to me.

I didn't even get the chance to do another scene, because now Monty B had decided he wanted to be Tarn Mandy said there was no point doing our scene again – so after break I had to sit there while Sam and Catharine got a *second* chance to show how good they were. I wanted to scream. It was so unfair.

At the end of the session I rushed out without saying goodbye to Mandy or Phoebe. I ran down the stairs to get away from everyone, but waiting for me at the bottom, with Jake tucked up in his pram and a big grin plastered across her face, was Diane.

"Hello, Polly," she trilled. "Look who's here to see you!"

I couldn't believe it. She was the last person I wanted to see. I pushed past her, out into the car park, and stormed up the road.

"Hey, hold on!" she called, coming up behind me. "Jake wanted to see where you get to on Saturday mornings. We got the bus all the way here."

I spun round to face her. *"What do you mean Jake wanted to see where I get to? Jake's a baby. He doesn't care where I go on Saturday mornings!"*

"Polly! Stop shouting for a second, will you! Okay, I'm sorry. Your dad had to go and do a job so I said I'd come and meet you. There's no need to be so rude." She took a deep breath. "Look, I'm here now, so why don't you calm down a bit and tell me about your audition."

"The audition was a disaster," I muttered.

"But I didn't want a big part anyway so it's no big deal."

"But you practised all week. What happened? Maybe your drama teacher will give you another chance next week? I could ask her if you want."

"I don't want another chance!" I yelled. I was so fed up with her pretending to be interested in my life. "I'm not even coming back next week. I'm going to call Mandy as soon as we get home and tell her I'm quitting!"

7
And the Part of Marcia Goes to...

We stood there for a bit glaring at each other in silence. I wasn't going to say sorry, if that's what Diane thought. I wasn't going to say anything. She blinked really fast a few times as if she was trying not to cry and then grabbed hold of the pram and strode ahead of me. I hung back taking little *pigeon steps*; heel-toe, heel-toe. I did feel bad about shouting, but then I never asked her to come and meet me at drama in the first place – and I certainly never asked her to steal my dad away from my mum and have a new baby with him.

"You must be starving, Polly," she called back to me in the end. "Let's stop and get a cup of tea and something to eat."

We squeezed into a little cafe on the high street, cramming the pram past the other tables into a corner at the back. I'd never been out with Diane by myself and I felt like announcing to everyone that she wasn't my mum. The last thing I wanted was for people to think we were related in some way.

She sat Jake in a highchair and gave him his big bunch of plastic keys to keep him happy, and then she ordered a cappuccino for herself, lemonade for me, and some toasted cheese and tomato sandwiches to share.

When the drinks arrived Jake went mad kicking his legs and banging the keys. He wanted the chocolaty froth off the top of Diane's cappuccino and she gave him little tastes from the edge of her spoon until he had a sticky brown moustache all the way round his mouth.

Diane smiled. "I shouldn't give it to him really," she said, "but he's just so irresistible."

She dabbed at his lips with her serviette. "What really happened at drama, Polly? Did someone upset you? You *can* talk to me, you know."

I shrugged and looked down at my drink. "I just think it's babyish. I've probably outgrown it or something."

"Well, yes you are very mature for your age," said Diane, sucking up as usual. "But why don't you give it a couple more weeks before you decide to leave? Your dad said you were great in your last production and I was really looking forward to seeing you perform."

"Yeah, and don't tell me, *Jakey was really looking forward to it too!*"

Diane looked at me sharply. I knew she was itching to tell me not to be so sarcastic but she bent down to pick up Jake's keys from the floor and when she sat up again she had a smile on her face. The same sort of false smile Mandy fixed on her face when Arthur came in to talk to her last week.

"I've got an idea," she said. "I've been meaning to discuss it with you all week. I know your new room is really tiny – no bigger than a shoebox really, but why don't we go to the DIY store this afternoon and pick out some new paint? Any colour you like. I really want you to feel at home while your mum's away and it's such an awful sludgy-brown colour at the moment."

She started going on about how I could paint the walls purple with silver stars or pink with gold around the edges. "Let's go right now," she said, signalling to the waiter that we wanted to pay. "It's Sunday tomorrow so we'll have all day to get it sorted."

I was dying to say, "What's the point?" I mean, I was only going to be there for another week or two. But then I remembered the auditions and Monty B's great performance and I knew he'd ruined my chance of getting a good enough part to stop Mum going to Spain.

I'd *have* to go back to drama on Saturday after all. I'd have to go back and beg Mandy to give me another chance. If she let me read Marcia's part with someone normal, like Sandeep or Adam, she might realize just how good I could be.

"You're very quiet," said Diane.

I stirred the straw round my lemonade. "I'm just trying to decide what colour paint I'd like," I lied.

I wasn't about to tell Diane about my big plan to keep Mum in England so I decided to go along with *The Great Painting-My-Room Idea* – if that was what made her happy.

As soon as we finished eating we hurried down to the nearest DIY shop and made our way over to the paint section. There were hundreds of different colours all lined up in neat rows. There were pearly-pinks and greeny-blues and at least four different shades of gold. I chose a bright green colour called Emerald

City Green and Diane loaded the tins into our trolley, twittering on about how it was exactly the same shade as my eyes.

So in the end I didn't ring Mandy to tell her I was quitting drama. I went back to Dad and Diane's and we spent most of Sunday painting my room. And, when I got home from school on Monday, Diane had bought me some silky, green cushions and a green and gold sparkly bedspread. And I carried on practising my scene to show Mandy on Saturday and Mum carried on getting ready for Spain and poor old Cosmo carried on waiting for me every morning; sitting patiently on the wall outside number 25 until I appeared at the top of the road.

Phoebe called round for me on Saturday morning. We were going to get the bus to drama for the very first time and she was so excited, she arrived before we'd even had breakfast. Dad made a big thing of showing her my

"Emerald City" room and Jake put on a special performance – rolling over on his blanket and then back again while Phoebe, Dad and Diane clapped and cheered. Phoebe made a massive fuss of him, pulling him up onto her lap and singing baby songs to him while she clapped his hands together.

"You were so right, Polly," she said. "You have got the most gorgeous brother in the world. I'd swap him with Sara in a second!" Jake squealed and blew raspberries right in her face.

"Did you really say that, Polly?" said Diane, grinning from ear to ear. She lifted Jake off Phoebe's lap and practically threw him up in the air. "Do you hear that, you little monkey... your big sister thinks you're the most gorgeous baby in the world!"

"I wasn't being serious," I muttered, grabbing hold of Phoebe and dragging her out of the room.

"What did you have to go and say that for?" I hissed, as we left the house. "You know I didn't mean it."

"I'm sorry, Polly, it's just that he's so cute and everything, I forgot for a minute that you made all that stuff up. Anyway, I think Diane's really nice and your room looks great."

I shook my head and sighed. Sometimes I wondered if Phoebe understood at all what a nightmare it was being stuck at Dad's with Diane and Jake.

"Anyway," she went on. "Do you think we'll find out our parts today? I know Monty B was messing about – but your audition was brilliant."

"No it wasn't!" I snapped. "It was rubbish."

"All right, I was only saying."

"I know, I know. Sorry." The last thing I wanted was to fall out with Phoebe when we'd just started to get close. I linked my arm through hers. "Who do you want to be then?"

"I really want to be Rainbow. You know, from the scene I did for my audition. It's not like a massive part or anything, but she sings a big solo – a whole song all by herself."

"Well, I bet you'll get it," I said. "It sounds perfect for you."

Ellie and Sam were hanging about outside when we arrived, so we all went up together. I was dying to ask Mandy straight away if I could re-audition, but she was standing by the piano talking to Arthur with that awful fixed smile on her face and it didn't look like the best moment to interrupt. A minute later Arthur strode out and Mandy called us over to sit in a circle.

"I'm trying my best to stay calm," she said. "But he doesn't make it easy. I only have to see that man walk through the door and my stress levels go haywire. Anyway, the latest with Arthur, in case you were wondering, is that he's somehow persuaded a local TV station to film his great ballroom dancing event."

"You mean they're going to be filming *here*? In *this* hall?" said Monty B. "But will it be on a Saturday?"

"Of course it will," said Mandy, "this *is* Arthur we're talking about. Any opportunity to disrupt our sessions! Anyway, I don't want to think about it right now. We've got a show to be getting on with and the dance is not for weeks and weeks."

Monty B was practically bouncing up and down in excitement. "But that means I've got loads of time to brush up on my ballroom skills. You never know who might be watching. I could be spotted! This could be my One Big Chance!"

"Oh my God!" snorted Neesha. "Your One Big Chance to be spotted by who exactly?"

"Well, for your information, I was dancing the waltz with my nan on holiday last summer and we won a medal for best pair on the dance floor."

"Yeah, but how many other people were actually *on* the dance floor?"

Monty B opened his mouth to answer, but Mandy clapped her hand over it.

"Stop!" she laughed. "I don't want to waste another second talking about Arthur and his blessed dance contest. We're going to go over the opening song this morning. Now that I've cast the part of Marcia we can sing it all the way through."

My head snapped up. "What do you mean?" I said. "What do you mean, *Now that you've cast the part of Marcia?*"

"Well I'm going to tell everyone their parts in a minute and then we're going to set the beginning and sing though the opening number."

"But Mandy, I really wanted to do my audition scene again. Can't I show you one more time?"

"There's no need, Polly. I've seen everyone

audition and I've cast the show. We haven't really got time to start auditioning again."

I couldn't believe it. "But it's not fair! Monty B *ruined* my audition, leaping about like an idiot singing Scooby Doo. I wanted to have another go – with Adam or Sandeep."

"Stop whinging, can't you?" Sam muttered.

"Honestly, Polly, there's no need," said Mandy. "I know Monty B was messing about but it didn't really affect my decision."

"But look..." I picked up my script to show her the scene I'd been practising, but just at that moment Arthur came striding back into the hall.

"There was just one more thing, Mandy m'dear," he said.

"Yes?" She fixed him with her fake smile.

"It's just that my partner for the sponsored dance was supposed to be Mrs. Beagle. She's marvellous you know – does a wonderful cha-cha-cha. But sadly – on her doctor's advice

– she's had to bow out; gippy hip or something. So, finding myself without a partner, and knowing how talented you are, I was wondering if you might be bold enough to take her place."

Mandy opened her mouth and closed it again. The smile slipped right off her face.

"It is for charity after all."

"Go on, Mandy," urged Monty B. "It could be *your* Big Chance. I can see it now. Arthur and Mandy – the new Bruce and Tess!"

Arthur did a few fancy steps and slid across the floor towards Mandy.

"What do you say, *Tess*?"

"Erm...I'll have to think about it," said Mandy. "I'll let you know later on today. We were right in the middle of something." She tried to put the smile back on her face but I could see the effort was nearly killing her.

Arthur slapped his own hand. "Naughty boy," he said. "Interrupting again. Come and find me in my office at the end of the session. I'll be waiting!"

We all looked at Mandy as Arthur danced out of the room.

"Oh, you have *so* got to do it," squealed Neesha. "You'll be on the telly and everything."

"That's exactly why I'm *not* going to do it," said Mandy firmly. "Now let's get on with casting the show. Following her fantastic audition..."

I closed my eyes.

"The part of Marcia goes to..."

I stopped breathing.

"Polly!"

Telling Mum

I sat there in a daze. I couldn't believe I'd heard right, but everyone was grinning at me and clapping; well, everyone except for Sam.

"You *all* did great auditions," said Mandy, "but it was Polly who really brought her scene to life. You totally convinced me that you were trapped and frightened and far away from home, Polly, so well done."

I was so chuffed I wanted to tell Mum right that second. I couldn't wait to see her face when I told her that out of the whole, entire drama group, Mandy had chosen *me* to play the part of Marcia.

"And it wasn't just Polly," Mandy was saying. "You were pretty good as well, Monty B. There was a great chemistry between the two of you – well, until you decided to add your own individual twist to the scene."

"Does that mean I'm Tarn then?" asked Monty B.

Mandy shook her head, grinning. "I'm sure I'll live to regret this, but yes, I do want you to be Tarn. But listen, you've got to promise to take it seriously – for Polly's sake as well as mine."

Monty B leaped to his feet. "I swear on Elvis Presley's life, Mandy. I'll take it so seriously you won't even recognize me. I'll be so serious you'll think I've been invaded by body snatchers or something."

"I wish you would be invaded by body snatchers," I muttered. I couldn't believe Mandy was letting Monty B have such a big part. I thought Adam was going to be Tarn, or maybe Sandeep. I was really looking forward to acting with one of them – but instead I was going to be stuck with Monty B *again*!

"Don't worry, Polly," Monty B said, coming over and putting his arm round me. "We'll be the dream team."

"Nightmare, don't you mean?" I said, ducking out of the way. But I couldn't help laughing. I didn't want to be with Monty B but it was worth it if it stopped Mum going to Spain.

Mandy read out the rest of the cast and it was brilliant because Phoebe got the part she really wanted as well. "You mean you actually trust me to sing that solo?" she said, her face turning crimson.

"Of course I trust you," said Mandy. "You've got one of the most beautiful voices in the group and you're so much more confident this time round than when we started the last show."

Catharine and Adam were Marcia's parents, and Sam was Cydore – the virus with the ability to replicate itself.

"Scary thought!" joked Monty B. "I'm not sure the world needs any more Sam Lesters."

"Very funny," snapped Sam, pulling a face.

Phoebe grabbed my hand, grinning. "Can you believe it?" she whispered. "I'm going to be singing a whole song by myself! How cool is that?"

"It's *really* cool, Phoebs, but I knew you could do it."

While Mandy was busy explaining to Sam why she couldn't have one of the biggest parts *every* time, I sent a quick text to Mum asking her to come and meet me at one o'clock. I didn't tell her why, I just said I wanted to spend the afternoon with her. When all the parts were sorted, we went over the opening scene and then we sang "Give Me Your Name – Give Me Your Number". I got to sing Marcia's part over everyone else and it was amazing.

"Try to learn the first five or six pages by

next week, Polly," said Mandy, at the end of the session. "You've got so many lines to learn, I want you to get on to it straight away."

"Don't worry, Mandy, I won't let you down. I'm so excited, I'm going to start the second I get home."

"Come over and practise at mine if you want," said Phoebe.

"Oh I'd love to, but my mum's coming to meet me straight from drama."

I hugged my script to my chest. I still couldn't believe that, out of everyone in the group, Mandy thought that I was the best.

"Well, I don't even think Marcia's such a great part, anyway," Sam announced, just as we were packing up to go home. "And besides, there's no way I'd want it now that I know Monty B is Tarn."

"Hey!" said Monty B. "I am standing right here, you know. Even macho guys like me have feelings."

Sam snorted. "Do you even know what *macho* means?"

"Of course I do. I wasn't going to tell you but Macho is actually my middle name, if you must know." He flexed his non-existent muscles and we all cracked up, even Sam.

"And this from the person who does the waltz with his nan," said Neesha. "I'd love to see what you're like when you're *not* being macho."

I left them arguing about how macho – or *not* – Monty B was, and waltzed downstairs to meet Mum. She was already there, leaning against the door, nattering to someone on her phone, but I didn't tell her about being Marcia. Not straight away. I was going to wait for the perfect moment.

"Your dad seemed to think you were going straight home when I spoke to him this morning," she said, as we walked to the bus stop. "You haven't had a row or anything, have you?"

"No, of course not. I just wanted to see you. I've hardly seen you all week."

The bus took ages and ages. While we were waiting, Mum tried out all her new Spanish phrases on me. "What do you think of my accent?" she said. "It's getting so much better, isn't it? Wait until I've been there for six months, I'll be fluent. Hey, listen to this," she giggled. "*Tenga cuidado España – aqui vengo!* That means, 'Watch out Spain – here I come!'"

I didn't know what to say. I hardly recognized Mum these days. She'd lost quite a bit of weight and had her hair cut and coloured and she did look better, but she was changing so fast I couldn't keep up. I was dying to tell her about getting the part, but she was so caught up with her plans for going to Spain that I could barely get a word in edgeways.

"Here, why don't you test me?" she said, when we were sitting on the bus. She pulled her Spanish phrase book out of her bag.

"I wish you'd stop going on about Spain all the time. Don't you care about leaving me at all?"

She shoved the book back and put her arm round me. "Oh, sweetheart, of course I care. I'm sorry. It's just that when I spoke to your dad this morning he said you were settling in so well and that you were getting really close to the baby. And you told me yourself that Diane has redecorated your room."

"But that doesn't mean anything!" I cried. I couldn't believe it. "Just because my room's a different colour doesn't mean I suddenly *love* it there – and I'm not getting close to Jake. I can't stand him, if you must know. He screams all the time and he keeps me awake and the way he eats is totally gross. I only said he was gorgeous for a sort of joke, I didn't mean it. And anyway it doesn't matter because I've got something to tell you."

She narrowed her eyes at me, frowning.

"What's the matter?" she said. "You're not in trouble or anything, are you? I've been so wrapped up with myself lately, getting ready for Spain." She took a tissue out of her bag and dabbed her eyes. "I've been really selfish, haven't I?" she sniffed. "Come on, silly. What's going on? You can tell me."

The bus trundled along. I looked out of the window, not sure suddenly if getting the biggest part in CRASH! was going to make the slightest difference to Mum's plans. She was so excited about going to Spain I couldn't really imagine anything changing her mind.

"I'm not in any kind of trouble," I said, still staring out of the window. I took the deepest breath. "I was just going to tell you that I'm Marcia."

"What do you mean, *you're Marcia*?"

I turned to face her. "You won't believe it, Mum, but Mandy has chosen me to be Marcia in our new show. It's the main part. She's chosen *me* to be the main part."

"Oh, but that's brilliant news, sweetheart. I'm *so* proud of you." She grabbed hold of my hands. "Look at me, crying and carrying on, when all the time you had this wonderful news. You'd better tell me when it is so that I can arrange to fly back. I wouldn't miss it for the world."

"Fly back?" I whispered. "What do you mean, *fly back*?"

But I knew exactly what she meant. Getting the main part in the show wasn't going to stop Mum going to Spain. I don't know how I could've been so stupid. How I could've thought that a tiny little thing like me having the starring role in the next Star Makers production could matter enough to make Mum change her mind?

As soon as we got off the bus I muttered something about scenes to practise and ran all the way back to Dad's. "Come and see Cosmo," Mum called out after me, but I didn't stop.

Diane was home. I could hear her in the kitchen feeding Jake but I raced straight upstairs and shut myself in my room. I lay on my bed for ages thinking about how my plan had failed. Mum was leaving and she probably wouldn't even bother to come back to see me in the show. She'd probably be so caught up in her new life by then that she'd forget about me altogether. I was stuck here for a year and there was absolutely nothing I could do.

Diane popped up after a bit to see if I was okay, but I just smiled at her and said I was fine. Mandy had the right idea. What was it she'd said about Arthur? *"I'm just going to smile at him and pretend he doesn't really exist."* That's how I'd get through the year. I'd just smile and say I was fine and not show anyone how I really felt about Dad leaving Mum, and about Desperate Di and The Great Baby Jake, and about Mum dumping me at Dad's so that she could swan off to Spain.

I must've dropped off to sleep in the end because the next thing I knew it was dark outside and the house was quiet. I opened my door and saw that either Dad or Diane had left a sandwich and a drink for me in the hall, but I wasn't hungry. I closed the door and settled down in front of the computer.

I hadn't played **THWACKERS** for days but when I logged on I saw I was still second on the leader board. The game wasn't even that great, but the more I played the less I thought about Mum leaving. I carried on until I could hear the birds singing outside my window. I sat there hunched over the computer eliminating one baddie after another while my score went up and up.

It was almost light outside by the time I'd finished. It seemed like ages since I'd been on the bus with Mum. In three days she'd be in Spain and there was nothing I could do to stop her.

A message flashed across the computer.

CONGRATULATIONS! YOU HAVE SUCCESSFULLY MADE IT TO THE TOP OF THE LEADER BOARD.

I wasn't even that bothered about being top, I just enjoyed playing. I tried to find another game but they all looked stupid. I searched around for a bit but there was nothing. I was just about to give up and crawl into bed, when I remembered that website they were all talking about at drama, friend2friend. The site Dad had forbidden me to go on. I knew he'd go mad if I even looked at it, but right at that moment I was too tired and too angry to care.

It was easy to find. It came up straight away. I sat there for a bit, my palms suddenly sweaty even though my room was pretty cold.

The screen was completely empty except for a sparkly silver door.

A message appeared on the door handle.

It said: "Click here to enter..."

My Perfect Friend

I clicked on the door and waited. Nothing happened for ages and I wondered if Dad had actually blocked the site or something. Finally I heard the sound of a key turning and the silver door swung open. The screen was blank for a second and then another message appeared: "Welcome to friend2friend, a special place for special people to meet, hang out and chat. Please click on the Sapphire door."

The friend2friend home page certainly didn't look particularly dangerous or sinister, but I was so tired it was difficult to think straight. It was divided up into different rooms and each room had the name of a precious stone. To go any further you had to click on the Sapphire door and enter your personal details.

I knew I shouldn't give out any personal information. Dad had warned me about that a million times – along with more or less every teacher at school – but I was really curious to know what was so special about friend2friend.

I wondered what would happen if I pretended to be someone else; someone with a completely different life. It's not like I actually had to say I was Polly Carter. It would be brilliant to be someone else, even if it was only made up – but what if somehow the computer knew I was lying? I was still trying to work out what to do when Diane called me down for breakfast.

"What, on the computer already?" she said, popping her head round the door.

I smiled at her as if I didn't have a care in the world. "Don't worry, I'll be down in a sec."

As soon as she'd shut the door I clicked on the Sapphire door and my fingers started to fly across the keyboard.

Name: Marcia Moon (Well, I was Marcia in a way.)
Age: 13 (That was the minimum age.)
Hobbies: Singing, dancing, acting, hanging out with my friends (That bit was true.)
Best friend: My twin sister Phoebe (I'd always wanted a twin!) and my cat Cosmo

The second I clicked "enter" my personal details were sort of sucked into the Sapphire room and I thought that would be it, but a minute or two later another form appeared with more questions. What school year was I in? What were my best subjects? Who was my favourite singer? The list went on and on. The last section was all about my family. It was fun writing about Mum and Dad and my fantastic twin Phoebe. And of course, we all lived together with our beautiful cat, Cosmo.

Eventually the questions stopped and a new message flashed across the screen.

"Thank you, Marcia Moon, your details have been accepted. Please enter your username and click on the Ruby door."

Diane called me again from downstairs but I didn't move. I didn't want to log off in case I had to start all over again. I'd never be able to remember exactly what I'd said and if I answered the questions differently second time round it would be obvious I'd made half of it up. In the end I minimized the screen and left the computer running.

"Morning, Polly." Dad pulled his chair in so I could squeeze past him to sit at the table. "What happened to you last night? You were spark out. Where did you go with your mum?"

I shrugged and helped myself to toast. "We didn't really go anywhere. I had lines to learn so I came straight home."

"Did you get a good part in the end?" asked Diane. "I know you were a bit worried." She looked over my head and mouthed something to Dad about the audition being a disaster.

"I wasn't worried!" I snapped, but then I remembered that I was supposed to be smiling my way through the year. "Honestly, I wasn't worried," I said again, doing my best to calm down. "And anyway I had quite a big part in the last show."

"Yes, but I thought this time you wanted the *biggest* part," said Dad, but before I could answer, he'd scooped Jake out of his highchair and was galloping around the tiny kitchen pretending to be a horse or something. Jake squealed and squealed and Diane clapped and Dad snorted and neighed and they were so caught up in the game, I managed to slip out with my toast and back upstairs to my room.

The friend2friend home page was still there and all my answers had been saved. I knew I should go to bed and get some sleep, but I was dying to see what would happen next. I entered my username as "Marcia2" and clicked on the

Ruby door and as the screen cleared a new message appeared. It said: "Welcome to the Ruby room, where you get to choose your perfect friend. Answer these few simple questions and we'll find you the <u>best</u> best friend ever!"

I couldn't believe it...*more questions*...but these ones were easy. I knew exactly what kind of best friend I'd love to have: someone who wanted to be with me all the time; someone I could share everything with – all my secrets and hopes and dreams; and someone who understood me – no matter what.

I forgot all about how tired I was and how gutted I was about Mum leaving. I described all the exciting things me and my perfect friend would do together; sleepovers and shopping and double dates. Camping and horse riding and West End shows. The list was endless. I was still typing away when Dad called up to say Mum was at the door.

Mum had never been round to Diane's – not

since Dad had left her to move in here – and for a fraction of a second I wondered if she'd come round to tell me she'd changed her mind about going to Spain after all. I bolted out of my room and down the stairs two at a time.

She was standing stiffly on the doorstep looking horribly uncomfortable.

"Hello, Polly, love," she said, her lips so thin they'd almost disappeared. "Busy practising your lines?"

I nodded, barely able to breathe, waiting for her to say the magic words; just waiting for her to make everything okay again. She took a tissue out of her bag and started to dab at her eyes.

"I've just popped round to let you know that I'm actually packing up today. Remember that nice couple Mr. and Mrs. Bay, who came to look round the house a couple of weeks ago? Well, they're moving in tomorrow, so I need to be out of the house by six o'clock this evening." She dabbed at her eyes again and I could see she was trying so hard not to cry in front of Diane. "I'm only going to be over at number 20. Tracy says I can stay there for a couple of nights, but the thing is, we really need to sort out Cosmo."

"That's fine," said Diane, quickly. She was standing behind me looking just as awkward as Mum. "Why don't you pop along with your mum and get him now, Polly, and then you can spend the rest of the day settling him in."

I carried Cosmo up the road, talking to him all the way. He started to wriggle and squirm as we came up the path to the front door at number 11, but I held on to him as tightly as I could, trying to reassure him that everything was going to be okay. The second we got inside he scrambled out of my arms, shot through the door into the living room – and straight under the sofa. He stayed under there for the rest of the day.

I spent ages lying on the floor trying to convince him that it was safe to come out, but he wouldn't budge. I even slid a bowl of his favourite food under the sofa to tempt him out – but it didn't make the slightest difference.

"Just give him some time," said Diane. "He'll soon learn to trust us. You know, I popped in to see the vet during the week and he said we should put some butter on his paws."

I looked up from the floor. "He said *what*?"

"No, seriously, Polly. I told him about Cosmo coming to live with us and he said if we put butter on his paws, he'd lick it off – and then, when he wanted more, he'd find his way straight back to where he first got it."

"And he knows that for a fact, does he?"

"I really don't know if he knows it for a fact," said Diane, slowly, as if she was talking to a two-year-old. "But I think it might be worth a try, don't you?"

It probably was worth a try but it was going to be impossible unless Cosmo decided to come out from under the sofa. In the end I left him there and went back upstairs to the computer. I finished describing my perfect friend and entered the details. A few minutes later a message popped up in my friend2friend mailbox. It was from someone called Skye. I had no idea who she was but we started chatting.

Skye said she was my special friend2friend friend. That the computer had matched us up because we were so similar. She asked me loads of questions but I didn't tell her about Mum leaving, or Diane trying to suck up, or Cosmo quivering under the sofa. I was Marcia2 and I lived with my mum and dad and my twin sister, Phoebe, and everything about my life was just about perfect.

Cosmo stayed under the sofa for the next two days. We knew he was venturing out at night because each morning his food and water bowls were empty. And we could tell by the awful smell that he'd managed to find the cat-litter tray in the downstairs loo.

Diane was trying to be patient about the litter tray but I could see it was getting on her nerves.

"We'll give it a few more days," she said at breakfast on Tuesday, "but after that he'll have to start going out."

"But he might not be ready," I said. "If you force him out before he's ready he might not come back."

She screwed up her face, shuddering. "I'm sorry, Polly, but it's just not hygienic; not with Jake crawling around putting everything into his mouth."

"Don't worry, Di, love," said Dad. "I've bought a cat flap and I'm going to sort it out as soon as I get home from work today. That way he'll be able to come and go as he pleases. No more poohs, I promise. The only poohs we can cope with at the moment are yours, aren't they, little Jakey cakey."

Jake kicked his legs and blew a big raspberry. I felt like blowing a big raspberry myself – right at Dad and Diane – but I kept my mouth clamped shut and sat there in silence.

After school I went round to see Mum. She was leaving the next morning and Tracy had invited some of her friends over for a bit of a send off. I wanted to see Mum off by myself – to say goodbye properly, but she said Tracy had been so wonderful to her she couldn't really leave her own leaving party.

"*Hola*, Polly!" she cried when she opened the door. She pulled me inside and threw her arms round me. "I'm going to miss my little girl so much, you've no idea." She pulled a crumpled-up tissue out of her pocket and started dabbing at her eyes, half-laughing, half-crying. "She's so fantastic, this girl of mine," she announced suddenly to all her friends.

"She's only gone and got the biggest part in her new show at drama."

Everyone cheered and said well done and Mum gave me another hug, and then she turned round to her friend Jaz and started blathering on about the little apartment she'd rented in Spain and how close it was to the sea. I could see she'd already forgotten all about me and my brilliant part in the show – and how she wasn't going to see me for weeks and weeks.

I didn't stay that long in the end. They were all drinking this Spanish drink called sangria. It was in a massive plastic jug with bits of fruit floating around the top and the more they drank the wilder they became. At one point they started dancing around Tracy's living room. "It's the flamenco," Mum cried, grabbing hold of me and practically whisking me off my feet, but a minute later she was in tears again, telling me how proud she was and how much she was going to miss me.

Back at Dad and Diane's I was straight on the friend2friend website and in the Ruby room chatting to Skye. She wanted to know how I was and how my day had been.

"Fantastic!" I fibbed. "Phoebe and I organized this party for our mum and dad's anniversary and everyone drank far too much sangria. You should've seen my mum dancing the flamenco. It was so funny I nearly cried laughing!"

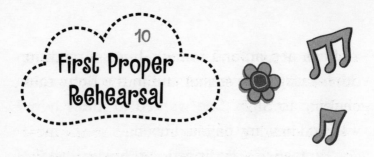

10
First Proper Rehearsal

I logged back on as soon as I got up the next morning. Skye was an only child and she kept going on about how amazing it must be to have a twin to share everything with. I got so carried away telling her about Phoebe and all the exciting stuff we did together that I almost forgot for a while that it wasn't true.

We carried on chatting until it was time for school. "Log on later," Skye said. "The more we chat the more points we get."

I didn't know what she meant but I didn't have time to find out. I ran downstairs and told Dad I was going over to Tracy's to wait with Mum until she left for the airport.

"Sorry, Polly," he said, shaking his head.

"You can pop in for a minute, but I don't want you missing any school. I thought you said goodbye last night?"

I just couldn't believe my dad sometimes. "You do realize Mum is leaving the country for a whole year? And anyway, it's not as if missing one measly day of school is going to make the slightest difference to anyone!"

Dad looked across at Diane, but I stomped out of the kitchen before he could say anything else.

Mum was up and dressed when I knocked on the door.

"Come here," she said, pulling me into her arms. "I'm so sorry about last night. I had far too much sangria. I think it must've been nerves." She hugged me really tight and I buried my face in her shoulder.

"It's all right," I whispered. "I know you're excited."

She pulled back and looked at me. "I am excited, sweetheart, but I wouldn't leave you if

I didn't think you were going to be fine at your dad's. You just concentrate on drama and learning your part and doing well at school and I'll be back before you know it."

I clung on to her for as long as I could, fighting back tears. It hit me, suddenly, that she wouldn't be able to give me a hug for weeks and weeks, and I didn't want to let go. I'm not even the huggy type, but then I'd never been away from Mum for more than a couple of nights – and even then it was only up the road at Dad's.

The day dragged by: double science and then maths. At lunch everyone was talking about CRASH! Sam said she'd already learned all her lines, of course, and Ellie was moaning about how she'd lost her script for about the hundredth time.

"It turns out it was never in that bag I left on the bus – but now I've gone and lost it again so I don't know my part at all."

"How about you, Polly?" asked Phoebe. "You must have loads to learn. Have you made a start?"

"Course," I said. "I know most of Act One already."

I hated lying to Phoebe but I couldn't tell her the truth in front of the others. Later on, when I managed to get her on her own for a second, I told her about Mum leaving and how upset I was. "She's probably on the plane right now."

Phoebe knelt down and rummaged around in her bag. "I've bought you something, actually," she said. "I knew you'd be feeling sad today, about your mum and everything." She pulled out a small package. "I hope you like it," she added shyly. The package was wrapped in delicate, silver tissue paper tied up with a sparkly ribbon.

"But it's not even my birthday," I said, giving her a hug.

"Yeah, but I know how awful it would be if my mum went away for a whole year. Come on, slowcoach, open it – I'm dying to see if you like it."

I started to untie the ribbon as carefully as I could but just then Sam and Ellie came bounding back over.

"You'll never guess what!" cried Ellie. "Sam just showed me her new socks and it triggered off something in my brain and I suddenly remembered where I left my script!"

"Down your knickers?" said Phoebe, giggling.

"Erm…in the dirty-washing basket, actually. I had five minutes to tidy my room the other day so I dumped it in there with everything else that was strewn across the floor."

"Hey, we didn't know it was your birthday, Polly," said Sam, spotting the parcel suddenly.

"It's not," I muttered. Now I wouldn't get to open my present with Phoebe – on our own.

"It's just a little present because Polly's mum's leaving today," Phoebe explained.

Sam sighed dramatically. "I wish my mum would go and live somewhere else for a year; she's driving me nuts at the moment. She's had this massive row with my big sister and it's put her in the worst mood ever."

"Come on, Polly, open the present," said Ellie, hopping about. "I'm dying to see what's inside."

But I shook my head and stuffed it in my bag, still wrapped. I didn't want to open it in front of Ellie and Sam. "The bell's going to ring any second. I'll open it later."

Phoebe's face dropped. "Don't you want to see what it is? I chose it specially."

"I do, really, but I'll open it at home."

The afternoon dragged by even more slowly than the morning. I tried to catch Phoebe at the end of the day. I thought we could walk home together, but she rushed off to netball practice with Ellie and that was that. An aeroplane flew over the playground and I wondered if Mum might be on it. I missed her already and she'd hardly been gone for five minutes.

I opened Phoebe's present the second I got home. It was the most beautiful photo frame with silver stars engraved all the way round the sides. She'd written a little card and put it behind the glass. It said, "I hope you like your Star Makers photo frame, Polly – well done for getting such a great part. Phoebe x x x"

I sent her a text straight away saying how much I loved it. I was sorry I hadn't opened it at school but I couldn't; not while Sam was gassing on about how great it would be if *her* mum went away. And anyway, it was supposed to be something special between the two of us.

I trailed downstairs to see if there was any sign of Cosmo. I could see he'd been in to eat but he was out again now. Ever since Dad fitted the cat flap he'd slip in when he was hungry and then shoot straight back down to number 25.

I spent the rest of the afternoon trying to learn my first scene. I said the lines over and over again, but every time I tried to memorize them I thought about Mum on the aeroplane and two minutes later I'd forgotten them again. It was just so difficult to imagine myself playing the part of Marcia when I knew Mum probably wouldn't be there to watch me.

By the time Saturday came round I still didn't know my lines. I sat by myself on the edge of the stage and read them through one more time; but it was hopeless. Phoebe was being funny with me as well. She hadn't actually said anything but she'd been a bit weird at school – ever since the other day when she gave me the photo frame. She was standing with Monty B and Rachel now, laughing about something. She saw me watching and waved but I looked back down at my script.

For the first hour we learned a new song called "The Rainbow Room". It's all about the game Marcia's playing when she gets sucked into the computer. The aim of the game is to get over the rainbow and reach the pot of gold – but the gold turns out to be a trap.

"It's a warning, really," explained Mandy. "Sometimes we waste an awful lot of energy wishing our lives were different, or searching for something, instead of enjoying what's right in front of us."

"You mean like the opportunity to be Arthur's partner at the ballroom dance contest?" teased Monty B. "You have said yes, haven't you, Mandy?"

"Well…I have said yes actually," said Mandy slowly. "But only because it's for charity, and I've told him I don't want the cameras on me."

"Oh don't worry about that," said Monty B. "The cameras will all be pointing at me and Phoebe!"

"*What!*" spluttered Phoebe.

"Well you *are* going to dance with me, aren't you? Come on, you know you've been dreaming about it for most of your life."

"Forget it, Monty B," said Mandy. "You're not dancing in the contest. The whole point is to raise money for charity, not to be the star attraction on the *Six O'Clock News*."

"And anyway, there's no way I'd do it," said Phoebe.

"What about you then, Catharine?" said Monty B. "I know you're a bit taller than me but you could always bend down a bit – or dance on your knees."

"No way!"

"Go on, Catharine," said Neesha. "We don't want to miss the chance of watching Monty B make an idiot of himself on national TV. *Or* Mandy dancing with Arthur. Have you started rehearsing yet, Mandy?"

"It's *local* TV, Neesha," said Mandy. "Stop

getting so carried away. And no we haven't started practising."

"I've actually been on TV already," said Sam, showing off just for a change. "I entered my cat Bella into the biggest cat show in the country and she was placed first in the older cat category. She got a rosette and everything. Hang on, I've got a picture here somewhere." She took out her phone but, before she could find the photo of Bella and her winning rosette, Ellie started to hop up and down, waving her arms about.

"I know, I know," she said. "Why don't we *all* enter the contest? I've always wanted to learn proper ballroom dancing and if all our parents come to watch we'll raise loads of money for the old people's home."

Everyone started talking at once, deciding who they wanted to pair up with and what dance they could do.

"Hang on!" said Mandy. "We can't spend

weeks and weeks learning a load of ballroom dances. I'm not saying *no* but *if* we all take part *I'll* choose the pairs and we'll spend *one* session practising. Okay? Now can we *please* carry on?"

She began to play the introduction to the opening number and everyone grabbed their scripts.

"We've wasted enough time already!" she shouted over the music. "We've got a show to put on in a couple of months in case you'd all forgotten!"

We sang right through the opening number *and* "The Rainbow Room" and then after break, Mandy taught us the dance to "Give Me Your Name – Give Me Your Number".

"How are your lines going, Polly?" she asked just before we left. "Have you made a start?"

"Yes, I've done loads!" I said, sticking a great big smile on my face. "I've been learning them all week."

"I bet your mum and dad were excited about you getting the main part."

I nodded, still smiling, even though my face was beginning to ache. I hadn't even told Dad. Every time I tried to talk to him about anything he'd start off listening and then Jake would smile, or reach out his arms, or start howling and Dad would be off. Pretending I was fine all the time was proving to be much harder than I'd thought.

When I got back from drama I went down the road to number 25 to see if Cosmo was there. The new family had moved in and it felt really weird knowing that someone else was sleeping in my room. Cosmo was sitting in his usual place on the wall but as soon as I sat on the doorstep he hopped onto my lap for a cuddle. "I wish you'd come home," I whispered into his fur, but I knew that as far as he was concerned he *was* at home.

I carried him up the road to number 11,

but he wasn't happy. "We've got to accept that we live here now, Cosmo," I said, staggering up the garden path. I took him into the kitchen and held him on my lap while Diane smeared butter on his paws. He struggled like mad but we managed to get enough on before he squirmed out of my grasp and back through the cat flap.

"Honestly, Polly, don't worry," said Diane. "He's just getting used to us."

She tried to give me a hug but I jerked away. I'd never get used to Diane or living at number 11 – so I didn't see why Cosmo would either. I trailed upstairs to my room and logged on to the computer. There was a message from Mum with a photo attached. I opened it straight away and there she was, standing outside her new apartment in the sunshine. She looked so happy I could feel a lump lodge itself in my throat and it was suddenly difficult to swallow.

"Hope rehearsals are going well," the message said. "Give Cosmo a big kiss, love you lots and lots – Mum xxx."

It was obvious she was having a brilliant time without me. She probably didn't miss me at all. I deleted the message and logged on to friend2friend.

"Where have you been?" said Skye, the second I entered the Ruby room. "I've been so worried about you!"

"Sorry...it's been crazy. I go to this drama club on Saturdays and I've got the main part in the show we're doing so I've been busy learning my lines. I've got hundreds! It's lucky I've got Phoebe here to help me."

Skye said she went to a drama club as well but that she'd never had the starring role. We chatted for a bit longer and then just as I was about to log off Skye asked me how many points I had.

"No idea," I wrote back. "How do I find out? And what are they for?"

11
The Emerald Room

It turned out that friend2friend wasn't an ordinary chat room. There were points and levels and all sorts of different privileges to earn. Every time I chatted to Skye we earned five points each and then another five points for every half-hour we stayed online. I asked Skye how come she knew so much more about the site than me, but she said I'd probably just missed an attachment or something when I first entered my details.

"We're working as a team now," she explained. "So the more we chat the more points we earn – and for every 100 points we earn we get to move up a level and gain new privileges."

We already had our first 100 points, so we were allowed to enter the Emerald room, and then when we reached 200 we'd be able to pay a visit to Pearl Palace and design our own personalized avatars.

The Emerald room was more or less the same as the Ruby room, except once you were in there you could chat to new people and earn even more points. I started to talk to a girl called Moose27 and someone called Tim. Moose27 went on about this band she'd been to see and what a nightmare school was and how her boyfriend kept messing her about and Tim told her to dump him and concentrate on school.

I didn't really say much at first, but there was something cool about chatting to a group of people who didn't know anything about my real life and I soon joined in. They didn't have a clue about Dad leaving Mum to live with Diane, or about Mum moving to Spain, or about how difficult I was really finding it to learn my lines.

We hung out in the Emerald room for ages and the longer we chatted the more points we got. Every time I thought about logging off, someone else asked me something, or Skye sent me a separate message from the Ruby room and I just had to carry on. I knew I should be learning my lines but I couldn't drag myself away.

I was still chatting when Diane called me down to eat. I gulped down my tea as fast as I could and carried on until bedtime. By the time Dad came in to say goodnight we still hadn't accumulated enough points to get into Pearl Palace and design our avatars, but we were close.

"You've been busy," Dad said, sitting on the edge of my bed and tucking me in like I was still a baby. "How was drama today? I still don't really know much about your new production.

Have you got lots of lines to learn?"

"Drama was fine," I said, my mind still fixed firmly on the friend2friend website. "I've got quite a few lines but I know them already."

"Have you heard from your mum, yet?"

I nodded and snuggled down under my covers, yawning. The last thing I wanted was to get into a whole big conversation about Mum.

I logged on as soon as I woke up. Skye was already in the Ruby room waiting for me and we chatted about nothing really, just so we could earn more points.

"By the way," she said after we'd been talking for a bit. "Why isn't Phoebe on friend2friend? It would be so great to chat to her too."

I made up some rubbish about Phoebe being a real swot, studying every spare minute for her exams, and changed the subject.

At school on Monday I tried to get the *real*

Phoebe to sit with me at lunch – away from all the others.

"I'll test you on your lines," I said. "Come on, we both need the practice."

"I know," she laughed, "but we've got to eat first." She sat down with Ellie, Sam and Tara and I slipped into the seat beside her. I just didn't get why she wanted to sit with them all the time when we could just as easily go off and sit by ourselves.

"My mum's still doing my head in," Sam was saying. "It's ever since that row with my sister. She spent most of yesterday nagging me to do my homework and then when I'd done it she kept saying how sorry she was."

"Sorry about what, though?" said Ellie.

Sam shrugged. "Beats me," she said. "Nagging, I suppose. I think she's having some kind of massive mid-life crisis."

"Maybe she's coming down with something," said Phoebe. "Like a cold or the flu."

"Well, I wish she'd hurry up and come down with it," grumbled Sam.

"I found my script in case you were wondering," said Ellie, changing the subject. "But by the time I got home that day it was in the washing machine and now it's completely ruined."

"Have you told Mandy yet?" asked Phoebe.

Ellie shook her head. "No way, I'm too scared. I don't want to tell her at all, not after last term when my *Dream Factory* script ended up lining the hamster cage. Remember?"

"Yes, but at least this time it's clean!" said Sam.

I listened to them talking away but I didn't join in. I was waiting to get Phoebe on her own so I could tell her about the message from Mum, and about how Cosmo was still running back down to number 25 every five minutes. But in the end the bell rang and it was time to go in.

"Why don't you come over to mine after school?" said Phoebe, as we traipsed back to class. "Monty B might pop round so you could start going through your scenes together."

"Can't you come over to mine, instead? Text Monty B and tell him to come to yours tomorrow or Wednesday."

"Don't be like that, Polly. You've got to start getting on with him at some point. Why can't we all be friends together?"

I scuffed my shoes along the corridor. "Just because our characters get on in the show, doesn't mean we have to get on in real life, and anyway, he won't want me to be there."

"Of course he will, don't be stupid. You get on okay at drama, don't you?

"Yeah, but only because we do all our scenes together. And anyway I've got to get home. I promised Diane I'd babysit for Jake so she could pop out for a bit."

"Oh, I'd love to babysit with you!" cried

Phoebe. "That would be *so* much fun. I swear Jake's the cutest baby. Next time Diane asks you, tell me and I'll keep you company."

When I got home Diane was in the living room with Jake. She hadn't really asked me to babysit, I just couldn't face going over to Phoebe's with Monty B. I tried to sneak past without saying hello but Diane called me in. They were crawling around on the floor together, but as soon as Jake saw me he stopped crawling and rolled over onto his back, kicking his legs in the air. I stayed where I was in the doorway.

"Don't ignore him, Polly. Look, he's rolled over specially." She tickled Jake's tummy, telling him how clever he was. "Watch him for a minute, would you, while I make a cuppa." She jumped up from the floor. "Do you want one?"

I shook my head and edged into the living room. Jake started to kick like mad and then he rolled back onto his front, and crawled over to me. I knelt down and picked him up under the arms. Sometimes I wished he was my *real* brother and not just my *half* brother. If he was my *real* brother I'd be the best big sister in the world. I'd look after him all the time. I'd feed him and bath him and play with him and do anything I could to help. It would be so exciting.

I used to nag Mum and Dad all the time to give me a little brother or sister when I was younger, but they would just laugh.

"We're busy enough looking after you," Dad would say, shaking his head. "How would we ever find the time for another?"

But he did find the time. With Diane.

I carried Jake over to the sofa and sat him on my lap facing me. He reached out and clutched hold of my hair, pulling my face down to his, squealing and slobbering all over me. I tried to unclasp his fist but he was too strong.

"Let go, Jakey!" said Diane, coming in

155

smiling. "He's got a grip of iron, that boy. How was school, Polly?"

"Fine," I said, smiling back. That's all I seemed to say these days. *How was drama? Fine. How was school? Fine. How are you feeling? Fine.*

And I was fine. Or I would be if everyone would just leave me alone.

I spent so much time chatting to Skye and the others in the Emerald room I hardly touched my script all week. I knew I'd be in trouble on Saturday, and even bigger trouble if Dad ever found out, but it was so exciting to see how many points I could earn. I carried on smiling and saying I was fine and pretending everything was okay and, in the meantime, I spent every spare moment hunched over the computer.

Dad and Diane nagged me to come downstairs and join in with them but I didn't want to, thanks very much. They were desperately trying to pretend we were one big happy family but it was such a joke. As if Diane baking a few cookies or Dad dressing up as a bear and taking us all on a bear hunt was going to make everything okay. I still hadn't told Dad about getting the biggest part in the show. I wasn't that bothered about it anyway.

On Friday night I stayed up really late chatting to Skye. We only needed a few more points to reach our goal of 200 and we were discussing our avatars. Skye was going to design a cute girly avatar with a funky hairstyle and loads of jewellery, but mine was going to be different. I hadn't decided how exactly, but it was going to be a sort of cat-girl with a studded collar and huge amber eyes. Her eyes would be so big she'd be able to "see" things before they actually happened.

"Imagine how cool that would be," said Skye. "You'd be able to win the lottery and stuff because you'd know exactly which numbers to pick!"

Yeah, and you'd know your dad was going to fall in love with the neighbour and that your mum was going to scarper off to Spain for a year – so you could do something about it before it was too late.

When I went down for breakfast the next morning, Dad was showing Diane an article in the paper about the friend2friend website.

"Have you seen this, Polly?" he asked, passing the paper over. There was a picture of a girl who'd got into some sort of trouble on the site. I could feel myself start to burn up. I was dying to know what it said but I pushed the paper away, shaking my head.

"Polly wouldn't be silly enough to talk to strangers," said Diane. "She's far too sensible. But you do look exhausted. Are you okay?"

"I'm fine. I just couldn't get off to sleep last night."

"Early night then tonight," said Dad. "And later on when you get home you can show me some of the websites you go on, just so I can make sure they're completely safe."

* * *

I could see I was going to be in trouble the second I walked in to drama. Mandy was busy setting up the stage to look like Marcia's bedroom, with a desk and keyboard and everything, and it was obvious she was planning to run the first scene.

"Can I have a quick look at your script," I asked Phoebe, grabbing her arm and steering her away from Mandy.

"I thought you already knew your lines?"

"I did learn them but that was days ago. I just want to make sure I haven't forgotten anything."

Phoebe gave me her script, but it was hopeless. I didn't know the lines well enough at all. I read through the first page and tried to memorize as much as I could, but I needed more time. I asked Mandy if I could use a script just for today but she shook her head.

"Why don't you have a go without it, Polly, and see how you get on? It's the best way to feel secure with your part, you know."

I climbed onto the stage and sat down at the desk. Everyone else made a line of chairs on the floor, ready to watch. There's this really long bit at the beginning where I'm playing on the computer and talking about the game, but I couldn't even remember how it started. Mandy kept prompting me but it didn't help. The odd word would sound familiar and I'd remember the next couple of words that came after it but then I'd go completely blank and she'd have to prompt me again.

"Polly, you don't seem to know it at all," said Mandy. "What's going on? You were so excited about getting the part, you said you were going to learn your lines the second you got home. I think you'd better come and have a chat with me in the break."

"Can't I just try again?" I pleaded, blushing a bit.

"No, just get a script for now. We need to get

on and I haven't got time to prompt you every five seconds."

Phoebe handed me her script and I started again but I still didn't do it properly. I was too upset. I didn't want Mandy to think I couldn't be bothered or to start wishing she'd given the part to Sam or someone else, but the harder I tried to get it right the worse it seemed to get.

"There's really no point in carrying on until you know it, Polly," Mandy said in the end, calling me down from the stage. "So who *has* learned their lines?"

Sam's hand shot up in the air. "I've learned all of mine!" she boasted. "I know I'm only a virus but I don't need to use my script at all."

So we ended up doing the scene where Sam's character, Cydore, replicates herself to trap Marcia and Tarn. She has to stand in the middle of the stage and chant in this creepy robotic voice:

"ONE AND THEN ANOTHER, WE COPY EACH OTHER... ONE AND THEN ANOTHER, WE COPY EACH OTHER..." And as she chants the stage fills up with more and more identical viruses who join in with the chant until it's very loud and menacing.

"It's going to be amazing," said Mandy. "The viruses will all be wearing these fluorescent green jumpsuits with green and black masks, and I'm going to hire a smoke machine so that, as the chanting gets louder, the stage will fill up with thick white mist."

"Golly, it's not real smoke, is it?" said Tara, alarmed. "You know how bad my asthma gets."

Mandy shook her head. "Don't worry, Tara, it's completely safe, but it creates such a great atmosphere."

Sam was brilliant of course. She knew every word and she acted like a pro, while I ran around the stage with Phoebe's script clutched in my hand, struggling to find the right place every time I had a line. Nobody laughed or anything but I felt so stupid and I knew I'd let Mandy down.

"It's okay," said Phoebe, when the scene was over. "I'll help you learn your lines at school. Why don't you just tell Mandy about your mum leaving? I'm sure she'd understand."

But I didn't want to tell Mandy about Mum going to Spain. She'd just think I was making excuses. In the end, when she came over to talk to me, I made up some nonsense about losing my script and promised her I'd find it and learn all my lines by the following week.

"I know you can do it, Polly," she said. "You were so good in the auditions. You just need to set aside some time and really get to grips with the part." She peered at me closely. "You do look very tired actually. You're not worried about anything, are you? Is everything okay at home?"

Her face was so kind and caring and I was so tired and upset, I almost told her everything. About Mum leaving, and Cosmo hating his new home. And how I'd only wanted to get the part of Marcia in the first place because I thought it might persuade Mum to stay in England.

"Well, there is something," I started, looking down at the floor and blinking hard to stop myself from crying. But just then Arthur burst into the hall and Mandy swung round to face him.

"Mandy!"

"Arthur?"

"So sorry to interrupt – it's just about the dance."

They started to discuss whether they were going to do a tango or a Viennese waltz and I slipped away over to where Phoebe was waiting.

"What did she say?" said Phoebe. "Did you tell her about your mum?"

I shook my head. "She didn't really say anything. I mean it's not as if we're performing next week or anything."

"Aren't you worried?"

"No, why should I be?" I shrugged. "It's only a stupid show."

Phoebe gave me a funny look but I buried my head in my bag and pretended to be looking for my snack.

"You know, Polly, I just don't get you sometimes," she said and walked off to the other side of the hall.

When break was over Mandy put us into pairs to practise our ballroom dancing. The competition was only a couple of weeks away and we still hadn't had a single practice. For some reason she'd paired me up with Monty B – she seemed to think it would help us to bond or something. Sam was partners with Sandeep, Catharine with Adam, Phoebe with Ellie and Tara with Rachel.

The others weren't so keen to join in so they sat in a group at the back of the hall and went over their lines. I probably should've sat with them so I could start learning mine, but I was stuck with Monty B, who was trying his best to explain the difference between a drop and a drag.

"Cheer up a bit," he said. "You should see your face. You're like that Russian princess who couldn't smile."

"What Russian princess?"

"You know, the tragic tale of Princess Polly who lost the ability to smile?"

"Don't call me that!" I snapped. "And anyway, you're the only one around here who's tragic. I don't know why Mandy keeps pairing me up with you."

"Well I wasn't exactly begging to be your partner either, in case you were wondering, but we might as well make the best of it now. Anyway, I bet *I* could make you smile," he said.

"Bet you couldn't. I'm not in the mood to smile, or laugh, or to dance for that matter – especially not with you!"

He grabbed me round the waist and pulled me towards him. "Just relax and follow me," he said. "I do the waltz with my nan all the time."

"There's no point trying because *we're* going to win," Sam called out, sailing past with Sandeep. They did look good – as if they'd been dancing together all their lives, but I wasn't about to let Sam be the best at *everything*.

"Come on then," I said to Monty B. "Show me what to do."

He tried to guide me round the room but I was rubbish. He said, "One, two, three, one, two, three," over and over again, but I kept stepping on his toes, and when he tried to turn me, I fell right over his legs and landed in a heap on the floor.

"Get up, Polly!" he moaned, pulling at me. "You're like a sack of potatoes. We might not want to be partners but we do want to win, don't we?"

"It's not me who's a sack of potatoes," I snapped, and pulled him down on top of me.

"Oh my God, yeah," said Neesha. "I know the show's called CRASH! but I don't think Mandy was talking about *that* sort of crash."

"Crashing is the new waltzing if you must know," said Monty B. "It's called the cross-body, reverse-turn spin-fall." He hauled me to my feet. "It goes one, two, three, turn. One, two, three, spin. One, two, three, turn. One, two, three, fall." He whisked me round and round and then tripped me up on purpose, pulling me down on top of him.

"I bet no one else can do it as well as us," he called out from somewhere beneath my tangled legs.

"I bet *we* can," said Sam, who couldn't bear to be beaten at anything, and she did a strange sort of spinning leap, dragging poor Sandeep round after her. They banged straight into Phoebe and Ellie who spun round and round before falling down as well.

"I think that's what you call a drop *and* a drag," said Monty B.

"Goodness me," said Arthur, who'd come in to watch. "I hope there'll be a marked improvement by the time the television cameras are here."

"And *I* hope we get to rehearse my show at some point in the near future," said Mandy, smiling through gritted teeth. "You know – the show that I'm supposed to be rehearsing *right now?*"

I got up and pulled Monty B to his feet. "That's the last time I'm going anywhere near a dance floor with you," I hissed. "*One, two, three, turn – one, two, three, fall.*" But even though I was trying to sound cross I couldn't help grinning.

"Told you," he taunted.

 170

"Told me what?"

He put on a ridiculous Russian accent.

"Zat I could make you smile ov course, Princess Polly."

When I got home Diane said Jake had developed a slight sniffle or something and that Dad had rushed him off to the doctor's. I logged on and told Skye all about CRASH! and how well I was doing, and by the time Dad got back with Jake he'd forgotten all about the friend2friend scare story in the paper, and how he was going to check my laptop for dangerous sites.

13
Mandy Calls Dad

The next couple of weeks flew by. I spent more and more time chatting to Skye. We easily reached our 200-point target and we had brilliant fun in the Pearl Palace designing our avatars. The more time I spent chatting to Skye and the others the harder it was to concentrate on my lines, or my homework, or anything else I was supposed to be doing.

Mum kept calling and she e-mailed me every couple of days, but I deleted the messages as soon as they arrived. I didn't take her calls either. I didn't want to know about her new job and her new friends and what a fantastic time she was having. If I didn't speak to her I could pretend she was still down the road at number

25 instead of miles and miles away living it up in another country.

I know she was upset, because she called Dad and tried to get him to put me on the phone, but I kept making excuses. She wanted to know why I was ignoring her, but it wasn't my fault. She was the one who'd decided to go off without me. It was so much better chatting to Skye – telling her all about Phoebe and the brilliant times we had together. Pretending I had a twin sister was like having the closest friend ever right there with me all the time. My made-up Phoebe *always* wanted to do the same things as me. She never had a go at me about anything and she certainly never wanted anyone else to tag along.

Not like my *real* friend Phoebe, who was *always* nagging me to learn my lines or to call Mum or to tell Mandy why I was having such a hard time. And if I ever suggested spending time on our own, she nearly *always* asked

Monty B to come along, or Ellie and Sam – so it was more or less impossible to spend any time with her by myself.

At drama, the ballroom dance contest was looming and everyone was busy selling tickets to their friends and family. I didn't even mention it to Dad and Diane. I mean there was no way I wanted them there watching me make an idiot of myself with Monty B. I was still struggling with my lines. I kind of knew Act One just about well enough to keep Mandy happy, but I hadn't even looked at Act Two.

"Why don't you just tell her you don't want to do it?" Phoebe asked me at school one lunchtime. We were actually by ourselves for five minutes because Ellie and Sam had detention for giggling all the way through science.

"I do want to do it – you don't understand. I just wish my mum was here."

"But she's not here, so why don't you tell

Mandy before it's too late? It's selfish in a way, you know, Polly, because there are other people who really wanted that part."

"What, like Sam you mean? Why are you so worried about Sam, anyway?"

Phoebe took a deep breath. I could see how fed up she was getting. "I'm not worried about Sam," she said slowly. "Why should I be? I just don't get what you think is going to happen."

"What are you on about? *You don't get what I think's going to happen?*" I was getting fed up as well.

"Look, Polly, Marcia's part is huge. And if *you* don't know it properly, and no one else is learning it *just in case*, then the whole show's going to be ruined."

"So basically you're saying that I'm going to ruin the whole show."

"Stop twisting everything!" she shouted. "I'm just trying to be your friend and help!"

She stormed off, shaking her head. She was

always walking off these days. I bet my *twin* Phoebe would never walk off and leave me by myself in the playground. She'd understand exactly how I was feeling about Mum and everything.

As soon as I got home I dumped my bag and ran down the road to find Cosmo. He still preferred to hang about outside number 25 and it still upset me to see him sitting there every day, waiting for me. I collapsed down on the doorstep and was just getting ready for a big cuddle when the door swung open behind me. I leaped straight back up and Cosmo went shooting under a car parked in front of the house.

"Oh, I'm so sorry, I didn't mean to scare him. You're Polly, aren't you? We met that time I came to look round the house."

It was Mrs. Bay, the woman who'd rented the house from Mum.

"He can't get used to his new house," I said.

I knelt down by the curb and tried to coax Cosmo back out. "Cats are like that."

"Some people are like that too," she said kindly. "I still miss my old house. Why don't you sit there for a minute and I'll bring you a drink and a biccy and then I'll make myself scarce. He'll soon come out once I've disappeared."

She came back with some chocolate digestives and a tall glass of juice. After a bit, Cosmo crawled out and I told him all about Phoebe and my lines and how she just didn't understand. Cosmo curled up on my lap and I buried my face in his neck. I loved sitting with him on the doorstep. It was the only time we got to have a proper cuddle these days.

I was chatting to Skye later on, telling her all about Cosmo and how special he was, when a message popped up in my mailbox.

"Well done," it said. "You only need 400 more points to reach your 1000-point target. Once you reach your target you'll be able to enter the Diamond Den – but from now on you must earn the points alone and not as part of a team."

"What's the Diamond Den?" I asked Skye.

"Not sure exactly," she said. "But it's supposed to be really cool!"

We carried on chatting for ages and when she said she was going to bed I begged her to carry on. I still needed another 360 points and I really wanted to find out what was in that room.

I stayed up chatting until really late and then, in the morning, I dragged myself out of bed and logged straight back on. I went into the Ruby room but Skye wasn't there, so I chatted to some other people in the Emerald room, keeping an eye on my points to see how close I was getting to my target.

I'd made quite a few friends on the site apart from Skye. There was Moose27 and Tim and a really nice girl called Pixie. Ever since I'd designed my avatar everyone called me Cat-Girl and they just seemed to assume that I was totally cool and full of confidence. Of course I wasn't like that at all in real life but it was fun pretending.

At some point Diane called me for breakfast. I trailed downstairs and told her I wasn't feeling well. I was too tired to go to drama – and anyway, I still didn't know my lines.

"What's the matter?" she asked, touching my forehead.

I shrugged her off. "I've got a tummy ache. I've had it for days but it's really bad this morning."

"Oh, you poor thing," she said, clucking round me. "I'll make you a hot water bottle to take back to bed. And do you want me to call Mandy?"

"Don't worry I'll text her and tell her I'm ill."

Back in my room I chatted on and off for

most of the day. Skye arrived at about ten and I gabbled on about any old rubbish as I watched my points creep up. Whenever I heard Diane coming I hopped into bed and snuggled down under the covers, pretending to be asleep. By late that afternoon I'd totted up another fifty points. My eyes felt peculiar and my head was pounding from staring at the screen for so long, but it was worth it. Or it would be when I reached my target. I had a short break and was just about to carry on when Dad came in.

"I've just had Mandy on the phone," he said. "Mandy from Star Makers."

I stared at him.

"She wanted to know why you weren't at drama today."

"Oh, sorry, Dad, I forgot to text her. I was feeling so sick this morning I just went straight to bed and..."

Dad waved his hand to stop me. He looked really angry. The angriest I'd seen him in ages.

"She also wanted to know if we were coming to the charity dance next Saturday. And most important of all – she wanted to know how you were getting on with your lines. She's a little worried that you don't seem to know them yet."

He paused for a minute but I knew exactly what was coming.

"Especially since you've got the main part!"

The Ballroom Dance

12

"For goodness' sake, Polly, why didn't you tell me?" Dad waved his arms about. "I kept asking you how the show was going and you never said a word. And what's all this about a dance?"

I pulled the covers over my head and tried to pretend he wasn't there.

"Stop being so silly. There's no point ignoring me." He crouched down by the bed and pulled the covers back. "And why haven't you been learning your lines? Mandy said you don't seem to know them at all, but you told *me* you knew them weeks ago."

I shrugged and turned away. "What do you care?" I mumbled. "I kept trying to tell you I had a really big part, but you were too busy with Jake."

He grabbed my shoulders and turned me back round, so that our faces were practically touching. "Look, I know you're upset about your mum leaving, and about moving in here with me and Diane and the baby, and perhaps I have been a bit distracted, but I'm not going to put up with lying. And what *have* you been doing if you haven't been learning your lines? Playing on that blessed computer, I expect! I'll take it away, Polly. If you don't start making an effort I'll—"

"No!" I leaped up. "I'm sorry, Dad, I'll learn my lines, I swear. I'll learn them all by next week and I wasn't really lying. I *was* feeling sick this morning and *so* tired, and I have tried to learn my lines but it's such a big part and there are so many and..." I trailed off. If Dad was this angry now I couldn't imagine how furious he'd be if he knew I'd been going on the friend2friend website behind his back.

He shrugged his shoulders, sighing. "We're all tired, Polly, it's not just you, and I did offer to help, remember, but you said you were fine."

"I know but I've had loads of homework, Dad, much more than last term. Look, I'll start learning them right now." I picked my script up from the floor.

"Make sure you do," he said, backing out of the room. "And turn that computer off for a bit."

As soon as he shut the door I chucked my script on the bed and sat back down at the computer. I had to get into the Diamond Den before Dad got totally fed up and stopped me going on to the friend2friend website altogether.

I spent the rest of the week chatting to Skye and pretending to Dad and Diane that I was busy learning my lines. Skye was so interested in everything I said. She always asked loads and loads of questions but I didn't tell her how cross Dad was, or how much I hated Diane. As far as she was concerned I was Marcia Moon and I lived with Phoebe, Mum and Dad and we never rowed or fell out or anything. We were The Perfect Family.

Dad called Mandy back and bought some tickets for the dance competition and every morning at breakfast he tested me on my lines. Luckily we never got very far because Diane was always asking him to change Jake's nappy or give him his bottle or sort out one of his crying fits.

On Saturday morning Dad made doubly sure I made it to drama and drove me up there himself. The dance was due to kick off at twelve, so we had loads of time to practise before everyone arrived.

Monty B grabbed hold of me the second I walked into the hall.

"Thank goodness you've come, Polly! The cameras will be here soon and we've hardly practised at all."

"Give her a chance to get through the door, Monty B," laughed Mandy, coming over. "How are you, Polly? Are you feeling better?"

"Yes thanks and I've started to learn my lines."

"Oh, that's great. From next week it's full steam ahead. No scripts and no excuses. Okay?"

I nodded.

"Look at this, though." She hauled over a huge, plastic container. "I managed to borrow some amazing outfits from the local fancy-dress shop." She yanked the lid off and took out one sparkly dress after another. The dresses were bright and spangly and smothered in sequins; just looking at them made me want to run straight back out of the hall.

"We don't actually have to wear one of those, do we?" I asked, shuddering.

"Oh come on, Polly, don't be such a spoilsport," said Tara. "You can't appear on the *Six O'Clock News* in your old jeans."

"I'm wearing this one!" said Mandy, grabbing a long, black tight-fitting dress, with a black feather boa draped around the collar.

"Oooh, very nice," said Monty B. "And this from the person who didn't even want to dance in the first place!"

"Well if I *am* going to be on television, I want to make sure I look my best," sniffed Mandy.

She shared out the rest of the outfits, leaving me with this ghastly, pink minidress covered in silver sequins. Monty B loved any excuse to dress up and he chose a sort of matching pink jumpsuit – it was just about the weirdest outfit I'd ever seen in my life.

"Aren't you embarrassed?" I said.

"What's to be embarrassed about? If you've got it, flaunt it! That's what my nan always says."

"*If* you've got it," said Neesha. "But what if you haven't?"

"Careful, Neesh," said Adam. "His middle

187

name *is* Macho, don't forget." Adam was wearing a black suit he'd brought from home and he looked great. I guess some people look good whatever they're wearing. Catharine looked lovely as well and I was sure they were going to win.

I went into the toilets to put on my dress. Phoebe was already in there squeezing into a frilly yellow skirt with matching top.

"I can't believe I'm doing this!" she shrieked. "What's Sara going to say when she sees me in this? I'll never live it down. I'm sure I said I wasn't entering the competition when Monty B first asked me to be his partner."

"You did! That's probably why *I* got stuck dancing with him!"

When we were all ready Mandy put on the music and we had a quick practice.

"Right," said Monty B, grabbing me round the waist. "You don't have to do anything except follow me. I'm leading, okay?"

"Okay," I muttered. "Whatever you say."

The practice went pretty well. I was determined not to let Sam and Sandeep win, so I tried as hard as I could to follow Monty B's lead and stay on my feet, and by the time we'd finished we were pretty good. It was the weirdest thing, but if someone had said to me a few weeks ago that I'd be twirling and whirling round a dance floor with Monty B, wearing a pink sequined minidress – *and enjoying myself* – I would've said they were bonkers, but it was actually the most fun I'd had in ages.

The camera crew were busy setting up and a few of us offered to help. I was just attempting to drag a pile of chairs across the room with Phoebe, when Rachel spotted us and came over.

"I'm really pleased you're back, Polly," she said, smiling shyly. "You're so brave to take on such a big part. I've only got two or three lines but I'm so nervous it's ridiculous."

"I'll help you with your lines if you want," Phoebe offered. "I was really shy last term, wasn't I, Polly?"

But before I could answer they'd skipped off across the hall together to grab their scripts and practise.

At quarter to twelve the panel of judges arrived: Mrs. Beagle, Mr. Hastings, the church warden, and Arthur's mum, Carole.

"This is going to be so easy," said Monty B, smiling and waving at Mrs. Beagle. "Mrs. Beagle and my nan go to the same knitting circle and they're like this!" He crossed his fingers to show how close they were.

"But it's not just her deciding, is it? What about Arthur's mum? She'll know we're rubbish the second we start dancing."

"We are *not* rubbish!" said Monty B. "What sort of an attitude is that? And anyway she can't vote for Arthur because that would be favouritism and Mr. Hastings looks as if he's about to nod off – so we're laughing."

I wasn't so sure but I didn't have time to worry about it because the audience were due to arrive and we had to hide away on the stage behind the curtain.

"I can't believe you're wearing that jumpsuit, Monty B," said Ellie. "It clashes so badly with your hair. I swear I'm going to get the worst fit of giggles in a minute." She breathed through her nose, her nostrils flaring out like a horse.

"Well at least you don't have to dance with him," I said. I had a quick peek through the curtain and saw Dad arriving with Diane and Jake. I was so cross they were there and that everyone was going to see them. I wished Diane would realize that I didn't want her around: especially not here in front of all my friends.

When the audience was quiet, one of the camera crew gave Arthur a thumbs up and he came out to talk about the old people's home and how the money raised was going to go towards buying a piano.

"What's happened to Arthur's beard?" Phoebe whispered. "It looks as if he's hacked at it with his eyes closed. It's completely crooked."

"Not if you look at him with your head on the side – like this," said Monty B.

We all put our heads on the side, laughing, as Arthur introduced the three judges, blew his mum a kiss, and wished us luck.

It didn't get off to a very good start. Ellie and Phoebe giggled all the way through their waltz. Sandeep and Sam were pretty good until Sam decided to lead instead of Sandeep and they ended up pulling each other in opposite directions. And then Arthur and Mandy had their go, but Mandy held Arthur so far away from her that there was easily enough room to drive a bus between them.

When it was our turn, Monty B took my hand and led me down from the stage.

"Our Big Moment at last," he whispered. "Just make sure you stay as close to the cameras as possible all the way through!"

I wasn't really nervous about dancing; I just didn't want to do it in front of Dad and Diane. As soon as Jake spotted me he started to go crazy, pumping his little legs and squirming about on Diane's lap – desperate to get down. I tried not to take any notice but it was impossible. Every time I turned round to that side of the audience he'd catch sight of me again and start squealing and pumping all over again as if he hadn't seen me for years.

We danced around the room whirling and twirling better than we'd ever done it before, but then, just as we were coming to our big finish, Jake finally managed to escape. He wriggled right out of Diane's arms and crawled straight across the dance floor.

"What are you doing? Go back to Mummy!"
I hissed, trying to smile and carry on dancing at the same time.

I could see Diane hovering at the edge of the dance floor ready to grab him back, but the other mums and dads began to laugh and clap, and Monty B, sensing an opportunity, scooped Jake up into his arms and swept him around in time to the music while I stood there like a total lemon.

The audience leaped to their feet cheering and Jake squealed and squealed and I could see Diane's face all proud and excited. The commotion even woke Mr. Hastings, who'd nodded right off. When the music stopped Jake reached out for me, wrapping his arms tight around my neck. Everyone came over to meet him, oohing and ahhing as if they'd never seen a baby before. And it was no surprise really, at the end of the competition, when Mrs. Beagle announced that we were the winners – all three of us.

Monty B's nan got so excited she leaped up shouting, "*Montgomery Bacon Brown, I am so proud of you.*"

"*Bacon?*" snorted Neesha. "Your middle name is *Bacon?* Are you telling me your parents named you after a bit of fried pig?"

"He was a very famous scientist and philosopher, actually," said Monty B, his face turning as red as his hair.

"Yes, and it could've been worse," said Adam. "They could've called him *baked beans* or *sausage*."

"Well I quite like it," said Phoebe. "I'm going to call you Monty BB from now on."

Sam rolled her eyes, smirking. "Phoebe and BB. How cute."

"You're just jealous that Polly and I won," said Monty B, grabbing hold of me and swinging me round. "There's no stopping us now!"

I tried to pretend I wasn't bothered about winning – that it was no big deal – but I was really chuffed. Monty B kept going on about what a great team we were and, for the first time all term, it felt as if he really meant it. As soon as we got home I rang Mum. We hadn't spoken properly for weeks, but I suddenly felt like sharing the good news. The phone rang for ages and eventually it went to her answer machine.

"*Hola!* I'm busy right now. Please leave me a message after the tone. *Adiós!*"

My heart sank a bit; I was so looking forward to talking to her. I left a message and waited for her to call back. I waited and waited but she didn't ring. I kept checking my phone but there was nothing – not even a text. She was obviously far too busy to bother about me. In the end I gave up and logged on to the computer.

I didn't care about Mum, or about winning a

stupid dance contest – or about learning my lines for the show. I couldn't even be bothered to go and see Cosmo.

I was Cat-Girl and the only thing I did care about was getting into the Diamond Den.

15

Hit and Run

Mum didn't ring back the next day or the day after. I was sure something had happened to her, but Dad said she was probably just busy working. I called her again and sent her an e-mail telling her to ring me as soon as she could. I began to imagine all sorts of terrible things and by the time she did call, late on Wednesday evening, I was convinced she'd been kidnapped by pirates or was lying dead in an alley somewhere.

"*Hola*, Polly!" she trilled down the phone. "I've just got your message. I had a few days off and we went to this *amazing* little island, but it was so remote I couldn't get a signal on my phone. Is everything okay? I did e-mail you last week to let you know I was going."

"Everything's fine," I said, remembering all those e-mails I'd deleted.

The lump was back in my throat and I was finding it difficult to swallow. I knew I should be relieved that she was okay but I wanted her to know how worried I'd been. I would've told her as well, but Diane was hovering about and the last thing I wanted was for her to start feeling sorry for me.

"Oh, Polly, I'll have to take you to this island when you come over," Mum went on. "It's like a little paradise; white sand and turquoise water. Honestly, I've never seen anything like it in my life."

She went on and on about how they'd been diving and how amazing the sealife was and then, before I could tell her any of my news, someone called out to her in the background and she said she had to go.

"I'm at work and they go mad if you make

personal calls," she hissed down the phone, and then she was gone.

I sat there for a minute, blinking back tears.

"At least she's okay, Polly," said Diane, sympathetically. "And she didn't *know* you were trying to get hold of her. I'm sure she didn't mean to worry you."

Suddenly I couldn't bear Diane talking to me like she was my mum; making out she knew exactly how I was feeling when she didn't have the first idea.

"If it wasn't for you she wouldn't even *be* in Spain!" I shouted. "If it wasn't for you I wouldn't *have* to phone my own mum to tell her my news." I was trembling all over. I was so fed up with saying I was fine all the time when all I really wanted to do was scream and scream until Diane disappeared. Jake began to cry, covering his ears with his hands.

"For goodness' sake, Polly, please calm down. You're upsetting the baby!" She came over and tried to put her hands on my shoulders. "I do understand how—"

"But I don't want you to understand," I screamed, pushing her away. "And I'm not going to calm down. I just wish you'd leave me alone. Everything was fine before you came along. I hate you so much! IT'S ALL YOUR FAULT!" I stormed out of the room and slammed the door as hard as I could. Jake started wailing behind me but I didn't care. I didn't care about anything.

I raced upstairs, logged on to the computer and typed and typed until my fingers ached. I told Skye all about winning the dance contest, but of course it was Mum and Dad watching me, and I was dancing with my twin sister, Phoebe. There was no Desperate Di, trying to suck up to me every five minutes, no snivelling baby Jake and no great big lump stuck in the back of my throat.

When Dad arrived home he marched

straight up to my room and said we needed to have a chat. It was obvious Diane had told him about our row, but I sat with my mouth clamped shut and refused to say a word. I didn't see why I should say sorry when it wasn't me who'd done anything wrong in the first place. He kept asking me what had happened, pretending he was interested in hearing *my* side of the story, but I wasn't going to fall for that.

"I'm with Diane now, Polly," he said in the end. "I'm sorry if that's difficult for you to accept, but she really cares about you. And you've got a little brother downstairs who adores you."

I put my hands over my ears like Jake does. I knew I was being a baby, but the last thing I wanted was to hear about how grateful I was supposed to be.

"It's about time you started to appreciate them instead of doing your utmost to push them away."

He stood at the door for ages and I nearly gave in and said I was sorry. I hate it when he's cross, but it was Diane who needed to apologize not me.

The rest of the week was a nightmare. Diane moped about the house with puffy eyes, her face all red and blotchy, trying her best to make me feel guilty. Jake was grizzly and unsettled, as if he could sense what was going on, and Dad was so frosty he was practically frozen. Cosmo hardly came in at all. I missed him like mad but instead of going down to see him I spent every spare moment on the computer.

Skye and I were both so close to reaching our 1000-point target that it was impossible to tear myself away. None of the people we chatted to in the Emerald room had ever actually been into the Diamond Den themselves, but they all said it was supposed to be incredible.

I didn't want to go to drama on Saturday but Dad more or less forced me. He said I had a responsibility to the group and that if I didn't go I'd be letting everyone down, but I still hadn't learned my lines properly so I knew it was going to be a disaster.

I tried to bluff my way through but Mandy realized straight away that I didn't have a clue. She prompted me a few times and then in the break she took me outside the hall for a chat. It seemed like everyone wanted to *have a chat* but no one understood how I was actually feeling. I stood there looking down at the floor, shifting from one foot to the other.

"I'm really sorry, Polly, I hate to have to say this, but I'm going to ask Sam to learn your part."

My head snapped up. "What do you mean?"

"I'm not going to give her the part – not yet. But I am going to ask her to learn it – just in case."

I tried to explain what was going on but the lump in my throat was so big I couldn't get the words out. What would I say anyway? That I was missing my mum? It sounded so stupid.

"I will learn my part," I whispered in the end. "I keep trying but..."

"Look, Polly, love, I'm not cross and I can see you're upset but you haven't really left me with any other choice. Do you understand?"

I nodded miserably.

"I'm sure it won't come to this, but next week we're going to run the whole of Act One without scripts and if you don't know your lines back to front and inside out I'll have to ask Sam to take over."

I trailed back into the hall and went to sit by myself by the piano. Mandy took Sam to one side and I knew exactly what she was saying. I could almost imagine Sam punching the air. Phoebe and Monty B did their best to cheer me up, but I said I had to learn my lines and buried my head in my script. I couldn't bear the thought of Sam taking over my part and I knew it wouldn't be long before she blabbed the news to everyone in the group.

Break seemed to last an age and finally, when everyone had finished eating and cleared away their rubbish, Mandy explained that we were going to spend the rest of the session setting the finale. In the last scene, Marcia and Tarn crack the secret code just in time, and as they're transported back through their computer screens, Phoebe comes on and sings her solo. Then, at the end of her song, we all come back onstage and do this amazing dance to the biggest number in the show, "CRASH!"

It was the hardest dance we'd ever done – a sort of mix between hip-hop and street – and I was concentrating so hard I actually forgot about how upset I was for a bit.

"It's way too difficult, Mandy!" wailed Tara at one point. "I can't even do *easy* dances!"

"I'll never be able to do it either," said Rachel, collapsing on the floor in a heap.

"Come on, guys," said Mandy. "I know it's hard but it's going to look amazing." She went over and over each little segment until everyone knew what they were doing.

There was a short instrumental section in the middle where Monty B and I had to dance by ourselves. Mandy sent the others off to practise the first bit so she could teach us our bit separately.

"Do you think I should learn this as well?" said Sam. "You know, *just in case...*" She trailed off, but it was obvious she was going to say, *Just in case I end up being Marcia!* She was like a vulture, itching to swoop down and snatch my part at the first opportunity.

"Watch from the front for now, Sam," said Mandy. "Polly's doing very well at the moment."

I was determined not to let her down. And determined to keep Sam Lester as far away from my part as I possibly could.

"Wow! That was incredible!" said Monty B when we'd finished. "You're a fantastic dancer, Polly – as long as I'm leading, of course. The cameras should've been here to film *that*!"

I still couldn't believe Monty B was being so nice. It wasn't that long ago I thought he'd never forgive me for the way I treated Phoebe last term – but maybe Phoebe was right and we could all be friends together.

"Oh, by the way, guys," said Mandy, "that reminds me. According to Arthur we actually raised over £300 for the old people's home last week. So well done, everyone."

We all cheered and then, just as we were packing up to go home, Arthur came in himself and announced that the dance contest was going to be shown on the early evening local news the following Monday at six.

"And I just want to say to all of you, especially you, Mandy, that I owe you a huge debt of gratitude. So if there's anything I can do to help with the production, *anything at all,* please don't hesitate to ask."

"The pleasure was all ours, Arthur," said Mandy, smiling brightly, but there was no way she'd ever ask Arthur for help – not unless she was totally desperate!

"Why don't you all come and watch the news over at mine?" said Phoebe. "We could have a Star Makers party. I'm sure my mum wouldn't mind."

"That sounds brilliant!" said Monty B. "And if you want, me and Polly could do a live performance of our winning dance right there in your living room."

Neesha rolled her eyes. "Oh my God, yeah, even if Phoebe lived in a mansion there's no way you'd ever be able to fit your head through the door. I swear it's so huge you're in danger of toppling over at any moment."

Monty B made a big show of toppling over at Neesha's feet and then before he could get up again Adam sat on him.

"I'll just try to squash his ego a bit," said Adam, squishing Monty B until he begged for mercy.

I left drama feeling happier than I had all week and determined to learn my lines. Even if Mum wasn't there to watch me, I still wanted to be in the show more than anything. I got off the bus and started to walk towards home as fast as I could. Great big giant steps. *I* was Marcia – not Sam – and I was going to prove to Mandy and everyone else just how good I could be.

I'd just got to the top of our road when I heard a terrible screech of brakes. I saw a man jump out of an old, red van, look into the road and then leap back in his van and drive on. I stood there for a second, telling myself that the road was empty, that he'd driven away because there was nothing there. But there *was* something there. I could see it as clear as anything.

I started to run towards number 25, my heart practically coming out of my chest. I knew what it was but I couldn't bear it. "Don't let it be him. Don't let it be him," I said over and over again, as I tore down the road faster than I'd ever run in my life.

But it was him.

It was my beautiful Cosmo.

Lying in the middle of the road completely still and covered in blood.

16
Diane to the Rescue

"COSMO!!!"

I stumbled over to him and knelt down. His fur was damp and, very close up, I could see that he was panting.

"I'm so sorry," I whispered. "I'm so, so sorry for not coming to see you *all* week." I didn't know what to do or how to get help. I looked around but the street was completely empty. I ran and banged on Mrs. Bay's door.

"Mrs. Bay! Help! Help me!"

I started to cry, I was so frightened. I didn't want him to die. Mrs. Bay wasn't there. I banged a few more times and then I ran back to Cosmo and cradled him in my arms. He was panting more heavily now – he looked like he was

dying. I was sure he was going to stop breathing at any second. I had to do something but I didn't know if I was strong enough to carry him all the way up the road.

I slipped my arms under his body. He was hot and there seemed to be more blood; it was warm and sticky and I could feel it seeping onto my hands. Somehow, I'm not sure how, I managed to lift him. I had no idea if it was the right thing to do, but I couldn't just leave him there. He let out a small groan; a sort of low throaty growl.

"I'm sorry," I kept saying. "I'm so sorry." The tears were streaming down my face. I couldn't go very fast in case I hurt him more, and it seemed to take for ever to get to number 11. I staggered up the front path and very carefully released one hand to bang on the door.

"*Diane, help me! Please, Diane, help me! Please!*" I started to wail. I didn't want to lose Cosmo.

Diane opened the door and I sank down to my knees.

"Diane, oh Diane, quick!" I sobbed. "Cosmo's going to die! Help me, Diane. *Please*. What are we going to do?"

Everything happened very quickly after that. Diane dashed back inside to get Jake. She strapped him in the car and then she grabbed her bag and a big fluffy towel. She put the towel on the seat next to Jake and then very, very gently she lifted Cosmo out of my arms and placed him on the towel. I squashed in next to him and we set off for the vet's.

"It's going to be okay, Polly," she kept saying all the way there. "It's going to be okay, you'll see."

The second we arrived Diane leaped out of the car and flew inside to get Mr. Adesina, the vet. He came running out after her and carefully carried Cosmo into the surgery. I was shaking by then. I wanted to go in with him but we had to wait in the reception area.

Mr. Adesina was amazing. He held up all his other appointments while he tried to save Cosmo. There were lots of other people waiting but they seemed to realize that it was an emergency and no one complained.

"He's in good hands now," said Diane. She wiped my face and stroked back my hair. "You were very brave, Polly," she said. "Carrying him all the way up the road like that. You probably saved his life."

We waited and waited. Jake got very excited crawling around the floor, playing with this noisy dog ball that had a bell inside. The receptionist didn't even get cross. She knelt down and started playing with him, rolling the ball from one end of the reception area to the next.

A few minutes later Dad came bursting through the doors. Diane had called him to come and meet us. Luckily he'd been finishing off a job close by. As soon as I saw him I started to cry all over again and when he asked me what had happened I could barely get the story out. We squashed up together on the hard, plastic seats and waited for Mr. Adesina to come out. After a bit Jake got bored and grizzly.

"Come on, you," said Diane, scooping him up off the floor and giving him a big kiss. "I'll have to take him home, Polly, but keep me posted. Let me know the second you have some news."

"It's all my fault," I said to Dad, when they'd gone. "I'll never forgive myself if he dies."

"What are you talking about, sweetheart? Of course it's not your fault."

"It is," I insisted. "It's all my fault because I didn't go and see him this week. I was so busy playing on my computer I didn't bother to go and see him and that's why he was in the middle of the road. He was waiting for me.

I bet he thought I'd forgotten all about him."
I start to cry again. I felt so guilty.

Dad turned me to face him. "No, Polly, love. He was probably chasing another cat or something. He probably saw something on the other side of the road and dashed across just as the van was coming."

I was about to say that Cosmo had never chased another cat in his life, when the surgery door opened and Mr. Adesina came out, wiping his hands on a wet cloth.

"I've patched him up a bit, Polly," he said, kneeling down by my chair. "But we're going to have to operate pretty quickly."

"He's got to have an operation?" I gasped.

Mr. Adesina nodded. His big, kind face was right up close to mine. "He's had a really nasty knock and he's bleeding inside. Unless I operate I won't know where that bleeding is coming from. Now, I want you to go home with your dad and I'll let you know as soon as he wakes up. I promise you I'll call however late it is, okay?"

Dad led me out to the van. I was still trembling and my clothes were stained with dried blood. Back at home, I had a steaming hot bath and then we sat in the kitchen waiting for the phone to ring. I kept thinking about how frightened Cosmo would be, waking up in a strange place, but Diane reassured me that Mr. Adesina was so kind and gentle he'd make sure Cosmo was okay when he came round from the anaesthetic.

In the end he didn't call until after ten. He said he'd finished the operation but he wouldn't know for a few more days whether or not Cosmo was going to make it.

"I've done everything I can to help him, but he's very weak and he's lost a lot of blood. I'll ring you tomorrow and tell you how he's doing and maybe later on in the day, after school, your mum could bring you in to see him."

I was just about to tell him that Diane wasn't my mum, but I didn't. I don't really know why. I suppose I was too tired and too worried. After that Mr. Adesina had a long chat with Diane and they made arrangements for me to come in and see Cosmo the next day straight after school – if he'd recovered enough.

It was awful at school, I couldn't concentrate at all and I kept getting into trouble. I tried to look like I was paying attention, because I was scared I'd get a detention, but it was impossible. I'd called Phoebe at home the night before to tell her what had happened and she kept giving me lots of hugs and asking if I was okay. She even told Mrs. Bliss, the science teacher, that I was in a bit of a state because my cat was recovering from an emergency operation. Mrs. Bliss didn't look particularly impressed but she did stop picking on me.

At lunchtime Sam and Ellie were going on about watching the dance contest on the news and how they couldn't wait to go over to Phoebe's the following week.

"Not that the result was fair," said Sam. "I mean it's obvious you and Monty B only won because of your baby brother, Polly."

"You mean it's obvious you're just a jealous pig!" I snapped, and stormed off to the other side of the playground. Phoebe came running after me and tried to pull me back.

"Don't be like that, Polly! She didn't mean it. I know Sam's a show-off and everything but she's okay when you get to know her. And anyway, why didn't you tell them about Cosmo?"

I shrugged. "I don't want anyone else to know. It's private."

Phoebe sighed and gave me a look. "What did your mum say about you and Monty B winning the dance contest?" she asked, changing the subject. "I bet she was sorry she missed it."

"I haven't really got round to telling her," I mumbled. "I haven't been able to think about anything except Cosmo. I can't stop picturing him lying there like that in the middle of the road, covered in blood."

Phoebe shuddered. "Well at least you'll be able to see him later today."

But when I got home from school Diane said Mr. Adesina had called to say that Cosmo *wasn't* doing very well – and it was probably best if I didn't come in.

"It's going to be okay," said Diane. "He just needs to make sure Cosmo's strong enough for visitors." But I didn't believe her and I started to feel sick.

"Can't we just go and see him, *please*. What if he dies and I haven't said goodbye? *Please, Diane.*"

Diane put her arms round me and held me close. It felt weird but I didn't try to pull away. "Listen, Polly," she said, "we have to trust the vet. He really does know what he's doing."

But Mr. Adesina put us off the next day and the day after. It was awful. I couldn't do anything. I spent all my time moping around, waiting for the phone to ring, convinced that Cosmo was going to die at any second. I knew I was driving Diane mad, but I couldn't help it. I just missed Cosmo so much and I was sure he wouldn't understand why I wasn't there to look after him.

Diane didn't complain at all. She made me one cup of tea after another and asked me heaps of questions about Cosmo when he was a kitten. I loved talking about him, it was really comforting. It almost made me feel as if he was there. I told her all about the day I got him. How Mum had picked me up from school and told me there was a little surprise waiting for me at home. And then when we got back she'd covered my eyes and led me into the kitchen.

"You can look now," she'd said, and there he

was; a tiny ball of fluff lying in this big furry basket. He was so small he could practically fit into my cupped hands. It was the most exciting day of my life – I'd wanted a kitten for so long.

Of course I never touched my script all week. I didn't even think about it. Diane asked me a few times if I was learning my lines and she offered to help but I couldn't concentrate on anything while I was waiting for news. Phoebe was great. She really did her best to cheer me up, but I spent most of the time moping about, willing the phone to ring. I didn't even log on to talk to Skye.

On Friday I came home from school and Diane was standing on the front doorstep. For a second I thought it was more bad news, but she was grinning, hopping from one foot to the other.

"What's going on?" I said.

"Hurry up!" She grabbed me by the hand.

"Now, close your eyes, Polly, and come with me."

"Why, what's going on? I'm not in the mood."

"Come on! Don't argue – just for once in your life!"

She led me down the hall and into the kitchen. "Keep going, just a little bit further."

"You know I'm seriously not in the mood for this."

She stopped walking and let go of my hand.

"Okay. We're here. Ta-da!"

I opened my eyes, blinking against the light.

"Look, Polly," said Diane, leaning down to Cosmo's basket.

And there he was, filling the *whole* basket, purring so loudly it sounded as if he had an engine in his tummy. I knelt down, trembling. Lots of his fur had been shaved off and he had a big plastic hood over his head to stop him from biting his stitches.

"Hello, Cosmo," I said.

And he pushed his face against my hand over and over again.

17
A Night Round at Phoebe's

I didn't go to drama the next day. I was much too worried about leaving Cosmo, for a start, but apart from that I still didn't know my lines well enough and I couldn't bear the thought of watching Sam take over my part. Diane tried to persuade me to go. She promised she'd look after Cosmo and give him heaps of cuddles, but I decided it would be much better to stay at home and take care of him myself.

He was feeling terribly sorry for himself. He absolutely hated the plastic hood, but Mr. Adesina said he had to wear it until he'd had his stitches removed in about ten days' time. He couldn't get through the cat flap either, the hood was too wide, so we'd gone back to using a litter tray. I thought Diane was going to kick up a big fuss about it but she hadn't said a word.

Phoebe called me during break to ask me what was going on.

"You should've come," she hissed down the phone. "Sam's doing your part and she knows *all* the lines."

"Has Mandy actually *said* she's going to be Marcia?"

"I don't know but it wouldn't surprise me. She's teaching her your songs right now, while the rest of us make masks for the viruses."

"Who's doing *her* part then?" I asked, quietly.

There was a long silence. "Erm...I am, actually," she said in the end. "I really didn't want to, Polly, I mean, why would I want to be Cydore? But Mandy said it would be a big help and I couldn't let her down, not when it's, like, only three weeks until the show. I'm still doing

my song at the end, but Rachel is going to take over the rest of my character's lines."

We said goodbye and I cuddled up next to Cosmo on the couch. I could just imagine Sam strutting about on the stage showing everyone how brilliant she was, but I couldn't believe Phoebe had gone along with it when she was supposed to be my friend. She called me again a bit later when she was back at home.

"Come over to mine, right now!" she said. "I'll help you learn your lines and we'll tell Mandy about Cosmo getting run over. I mean it's not like she's going to get cross with you if she knows what's been going on. I nearly told her myself but I wasn't sure if you wanted me to or not."

"Look, forget it, Phoebe. I'm so sick of talking about it. I don't even care about Sam doing my part. It's just not a big deal."

Phoebe snorted down the phone. "I don't believe that for a second. I don't know why you're being so stupid about all of this. It's obvious you still want to be Marcia even if you won't admit it. Anyway, you are coming over to mine on Monday, aren't you? To watch the news programme?"

"Course," I said, though the last the thing I wanted was to spend the evening with Sam while she gloated about taking over my part.

I was so hacked off with everything I went up to my room and spent the next couple of hours chatting to Skye. I told her all about Cosmo, but not about the accident. I didn't want to think about that, so I told her that Phoebe and I had entered him in the biggest cat show in the country – and that he'd won first place, just like Sam's cat, Bella.

"It was so exciting, Skye, you wouldn't believe it. He got this beautiful silky red rosette and the biggest silver cup you've ever seen and he purred all the way home, as if he actually knew how well he'd done."

Skye's mum wouldn't let her get a pet – not

even a hamster or a rabbit – so I knew she thought I was the luckiest girl alive. It was amazing, but the second I logged on to the friend2friend website and began chatting to Skye, I was so focused on what we were talking about I forgot all about Dad and Diane – and Mum not being around. And about how Sam had stolen my part in the show. I was Cat-Girl and my life was perfect and none of that other stuff seemed to matter at all.

"You'll never guess what," Skye wrote, when I'd finished telling her all about Cosmo and the cat show. "I've actually been inside the Diamond Den."

My hands started to tremble over the keys. I couldn't believe she'd let me go on and on about Cosmo when she had something so exciting to say. "OMG! What's in there?" I typed. "What's it like?" I held my breath waiting for her reply. It seemed to take an age.

"I can't tell you," she answered at last. "Not

until you've reached your target. But it's so worth it, believe me."

"What's the big mystery?" I wrote back. I was dying to know more but she logged off suddenly and a screen popped up saying I wouldn't be able to talk to her until I had enough points to enter the Diamond Den myself. I only needed thirty-five and I was desperate to carry on, but just then Diane called me down to help out with Jake.

"I've got to pop next door for a minute," she said, pulling on her jacket. "You don't mind watching him, do you?"

I did, but I didn't say anything. I've come to realize that when Diane asks me to do something for Jake, she's not really expecting an answer!

Jake was sitting on the floor playing with his shape-sorting cube. He had my beanie-bear, Boo, clutched in one hand and a red triangle in the other. He was concentrating really hard trying to get the triangle into the matching hole in the cube, but the second he saw me he dropped everything and came crawling over.

I pulled him onto my lap and we sat there for a bit stroking Cosmo. He'd been very gentle with Cosmo since the accident, rubbing his ears and tickling his tummy, almost as if he understood how careful he had to be. And even if Cosmo *wanted* to get away and hide under the couch, he couldn't fit – not with his plastic hood. *We're both trapped here now, Cosmo*, I thought to myself, but just at that moment he didn't look as if he minded one little bit.

When Jake started to fidget I took him back over to the shape sorter. He clutched the shapes in his podgy little hands, trying so hard to squash them through the holes, and every time he managed to get one right I clapped and cheered and he bounced up and down on his bottom squealing in delight.

"Polly, you're so good with Jake," said Diane when she came back in. "Honestly, it's such a help having you here."

I shrugged and moved back over to Cosmo. I hated it when she said stuff like that.

"He looks like you too," she went on. "He's got your eyes."

I shook my head. "No he hasn't! He doesn't look anything like me!"

Diane put her head on one side and folded her arms. "He *has* got your eyes, Polly Carter, they're green and they flash when he gets cross, you must have noticed. Let's just hope he hasn't inherited your stubborn streak as well."

She grinned at me to show she was joking. She'd been so nice since Cosmo got run over and I couldn't help feeling bad, in a way, that the accident had happened straight after that horrid row when I'd told her I hated her. I thought maybe I should say sorry, or thank her for saving Cosmo's life, but just then Dad came home.

"I'm back!" he called from the hallway. He kicked his boots off and popped his head round the door.

"What a sight," he said, in the sickliest voice. "My gorgeous family all together."

He gave Diane a soppy look and my stomach twisted up. I didn't want to be part of *their* gorgeous family. Mum was my family – not Diane and Jake. It should've been me and Mum and Dad living together at number 25.

Later on, at tea, Dad carried on with the happy families routine, going on about how great it would be to watch the news together on Monday evening.

"We could get pizzas and something yummy for pudding," he said. "Only ten months old," he went on, turning to Jake, "and a television star already."

Jake blew a raspberry at him and banged

his spoon. But I wasn't ready to play happy families and the thought of going round to Phoebe's for the night, even *if* Sam was there, suddenly seemed a whole lot more appealing than it had earlier that afternoon.

I didn't get a chance to go on the computer and get up to my target before Monday. Dad said I could only watch the news round at Phoebe's if I'd finished all my homework, and I'd spent so much time chatting to Skye that I was behind with more or less everything. I was still trying to wade through it on Monday after school, when Diane popped her head round the door and said I could leave the rest and go.

Ellie, Sam and Tara were already there when I arrived. Sam was all glammed up, wearing a really short skirt and high-heeled boots. The second Sandeep walked in she practically rugby tackled me out of the way to make sure she got to sit next to him on the couch.

"Hey, watch it!" I said, glaring at her, but she was too busy flirting to take any notice.

Phoebe's mum had made great big bowls of buttery popcorn and she gave us each a can of fizzy orange. I squashed up on the sofa with Phoebe, Ellie, Sam and Sandeep, while Neesha and Monty B and the others sat around on the floor.

We had to wait for ages until it came on. There was all the proper news first and then the business news and even the weather. And then, finally, when there were only a few minutes left, the presenter said:

"When Arthur McDermott decided the old folk at Cranberry needed a new piano, he organized a good old-fashioned dance contest to raise the money. But what he didn't know was that the real winner would be a ten-month old baby. Our reporter, Melanie Burton went along to find out more..."

"It's about to start! It's about to start!" squealed Phoebe's sister Sara, leaping up. She pressed record on the DVD player so we could watch it back later – and switched off the lights.

Suddenly, Arthur was on the screen bleating on for a bit about the old people's home and how desperate they were for a piano. He kept tugging on his crooked beard and at one point he dislodged a big flake of croissant. The camera followed it this way and that, as it floated all the way down to the floor, and then just as he started to explain the importance of supporting local causes, the camera cut to the dance floor. I groaned and covered my face with my hands.

"This is *so* embarrassing," I said, squirming. "I can't bear to watch. Tell me when it's over."

"What are you talking about? We were brilliant, Polly!" cried Monty B, turning round and pulling my hands off my face.

"Do me a favour!" scoffed Sam. "You only won because of Polly's brother."

And then suddenly we were there, spinning around in our glittery, pink costumes, right in the middle of the screen. And then, after a few seconds, the camera panned across to Diane and Jake and as Jake struggled to get down from her lap the reporter said, "And this is where it gets really interesting, folks. Keep your eyes glued to that baby!"

And the camera followed Jake as he crawled across the dance floor. We watched as Monty B scooped him up and twirled him round and everyone clapped and cheered. Then, a second later, the camera cut again – to Diane.

"I just couldn't stop him," she said, grinning. "He adores his big sister. And she's fantastic with him too. He couldn't wish for a better sister than Polly. We all love her to bits."

I sat there in the dark, burning up. I couldn't believe Diane had said something so nice in front of *so* many people. Suddenly Sara turned on the light and it felt like everyone was staring at me.

"Oh, that was so cute!" said Ellie.

"I wish I had a little baby brother like Jake, instead of a great big lump of a sister like Phoebe," said Sara.

"Shut up, Sara!" said Phoebe. "You're lucky I'm even letting you watch with us!"

"Hang on a minute," said Monty B. "Why is everyone going on about how cute Polly's baby brother is? What about me?"

"What *about* you?" snorted Neesha. "You're about as cute as a baboon's bottom."

"That's a bit insulting to the baboon, isn't it?" said Adam, and we all fell about laughing.

And then we watched the recording over and over again, getting sillier and sillier each time it came on. Adam and Sandeep started to lope around the room pretending to be baboons – shaking their bottoms in Monty B's face, so when Phoebe's mum popped her head round the door and said, "What's going on in here? It sounds as if you're at the zoo," I laughed so hard I nearly wet myself. I was having such a good time I forgot all about the friend2friend website and the Diamond Den. I even forgot about how much I hated living at Dad and Diane's. I looked around at everyone from Star Makers and suddenly the only thing that *really* mattered was getting back my part in the show.

And I knew exactly what I had to do.

18
Too Late

I started learning my lines the second I got home. I lay in bed reading the script over and over, memorizing each scene, until Dad came in to turn my light out.

"Mum called while you were out," he said, taking the script out of my hand. "She really wanted to talk to you. She said she had some news."

I sat up and grabbed Dad's arm. "Is she coming back? Is that the news? What about Mrs. Bay renting the house? Where will we live?"

Dad sighed. "Calm down, Polly. She probably just wanted a chat, but I'm sure she'll call back tomorrow."

She did call back, first thing the next morning. She'd been promoted at work and she wanted me to be the first to know.

"You mean you're not coming back?" I said, clutching the receiver so tight my hand turned white.

"Not yet, silly," she said. "I've just been promoted. But it won't be long, I promise."

When I'd said goodbye and hung up, Diane asked me if I'd had a nice time round at Phoebe's. It was so embarrassing, because she obviously knew I'd heard her tell the whole, entire world that she loved me to bits. I mumbled something about how funny it was when Adam compared Monty B's face to a baboon's bottom. But then Jake started fussing and by the time she'd sorted him out the moment had passed.

I waited for Phoebe outside school and as soon as she arrived I grabbed her and pulled her into the toilets.

"Listen, I need your help, Phoebs." I lowered my voice in case Sam or Ellie were hanging about. "I've decided I really, really want to be Marcia, more than anything, but I'll have to know my lines back to front if I'm ever going to convince Mandy. I spent ages learning them last night but I've still got loads to do."

Phoebe was so excited and tested me all through break and lunch and when Sam and Ellie came over to ask what we were doing we stuffed the script into my bag and she made up some rubbish about this science project we were working on for Mrs. Bliss.

"By the way, Polly, did Phoebe tell you what happened on Saturday?" said Sam. "You know, about *me* being Marcia?"

"Well, you don't know if you're actually going to *be* Marcia," said Phoebe, quickly. "Mandy only asked you to read her part *just in case*."

"That was to start off with, but then when you didn't turn up, Polly, Mandy said there was a very good chance that I'd have to do it for real."

"A very good *chance*," I said. "But that's all. You're not getting your hands on my part *that* easily!"

I walked off with my head in the air, but inside I was shaking like a jelly.

"Hey, wait for me!" shouted Phoebe, catching up with me. "You're not upset, are you?"

"Not really. Just more determined than ever to show Mandy that I *can* learn my lines."

Phoebe sighed. "I wish you'd tell Mandy about Cosmo – *and* tell Sam too. Honestly, Polly, why are you making this so difficult? Mandy would understand. They both would. You know how much Sam loves her cat. She's always going on about how beautiful and clever she is."

But I didn't want to tell them about the accident. I wanted Mandy to let me be Marcia because I was the best person to play the part, not because she felt sorry for me. I didn't want everyone going round saying, *"Poor Polly Carter – first her mum dumps her at her dad's to go off to Spain for a year, and then as if that wasn't bad enough, her cat gets squashed half to death under a van!"*

I carried on learning my lines all week and by Friday night I was pretty sure I knew them well enough to convince Mandy. I practised and practised until I could more or less say them in my sleep. I *was* Marcia, trapped inside The Rainbow Room game with Tarn, having one amazing adventure after another.

I couldn't wait to get to drama. There was only a week to go until the dress rehearsal and I knew we'd be running right through with no scripts.

The first person I saw when I walked into the hall was Sam. She had that smug look on her face but I didn't let it put me off.

"I'm back," I called out to Mandy. She was

busy sorting out the costumes on the stage and she had her back to me. "I'm back, Mandy," I said again, "and I know *all* my lines."

Mandy turned round, frowning. "Oh, hello, Polly," she said. "It's really good to see you but we need to have a little chat."

I started to feel a bit sick. Sick of people having *little chats* with me! She climbed down off the stage and led me over to the piano. I could feel Sam staring at me; her eyes boring into the back of my neck.

Mandy held my hands tight and looked me right in the eye.

"I don't know what's been going on with you, Polly," she said. "But it doesn't seem to me as if you've taken your part in the show very seriously."

"I know but...but..." I struggled to find the right words but it was hopeless. I couldn't even think properly let alone string a sentence together.

"If there is a problem, something you're worried about, you can always come to me. I can't promise I'll be able to help but I can try."

I shook my head. "There isn't a problem," I muttered. "I'm fine."

Mandy sighed. "The thing is, when you have a big part in a show, *the main part*, it's a responsibility – I thought I'd made that clear the last time we spoke. And I did keep giving you chances," she added gently. "And you kept promising me you'd learn the lines – I even spoke to your dad, remember?"

I nodded miserably.

"So when you didn't turn up on Saturday I had to ask Sam to read your part. I didn't want to, Polly, but you didn't really leave me any other choice."

I stared at the floor, blinking furiously to stop myself from crying. I wanted to turn round and run out of the room but Mandy hadn't finished. "It's a little bit complicated," she went on, "because Phoebe's going to do Sam's part and Rachel is going to do Phoebe's. But it's not as bad as it sounds. You'll still be able to sing in all the chorus numbers and I really am happy to see you here today." She stopped speaking and squeezed my hands. "Are you okay, Polly?"

I nodded again, even though I wasn't okay at all. I wanted to go home. I wanted to walk out and never come back, but I didn't have the guts.

The session seemed to last for days. First of all, Mandy got everyone to try on their costumes to make sure they were okay before the dress rehearsal. Marcia's costume was pretty plain, because she was just an ordinary girl sitting at home playing on her computer, but some of the others were incredible. They all rushed off to the toilets but I just sat at the side not really sure what I was supposed to be doing.

"Don't worry, Polly, I'll sort you out a virus costume for next week," said Mandy. "I've got a couple of spares here but I'll have to adjust the size." I felt like a virus all right, sitting there all by myself. Like I had some deadly disease and everyone had been ordered to stay as far away from me as possible, just in case they caught it.

When Mandy had finished adjusting the costumes and they were all packed away, we ran through the whole show, stopping and starting and doing bits over and over, and it was a nightmare. Sam was strutting about as if she was in charge of the entire production. Phoebe looked as if she was going to burst out crying at any minute and Rachel kept saying how sorry she was, and how she didn't even *want* Phoebe's part because it was only her first show and she was horribly nervous.

Monty B was the only one who tried to cheer me up.

"I'm going to start a campaign!" he announced at break. "The Give Polly Her Part Back campaign. I'll get thousands of people to sign a petition and we'll take it to the Prime Minister! The Queen! Anyone who will listen!"

"I've never heard of *anyone* listening to a baboon's bottom," said Adam.

"How about you, Sam?" said Monty B, ignoring Adam. "You'll sign, won't you?"

Sam didn't answer, she just gave him a look, but then just before we packed up to leave she came over to me with this horribly smug look on her face.

"Really sorry about your part, Polly," she said, sarcastically. "But I guess Mandy felt she *had* to choose someone she could rely on."

"It's fine," I said through gritted teeth. "It's not like I wanted the crummy part anyway."

She was talking to me just like I used to talk to Phoebe last term; pretending she was sorry when it was obvious she didn't care at all. But she was right in a way. Mandy *did* need someone she could rely on and she *had* given me loads of chances. It wouldn't matter how many people signed Monty B's petition – I'd blown it.

Mandy tried to give me some tickets before I went home but I said I didn't want them. She'd handed them out the week before and apparently they were selling like mad, but it's not as if I was going to ask Dad and Diane to come and see Sam Lester playing *my* part!

As soon as I got home I logged straight on to friend2friend. I only needed thirty more points to reach my target and I chatted and chatted until my head was fit to burst. Phoebe texted me a few times but I didn't text back. I didn't care about Star Makers or about Sam pinching my part – the only thing I cared about was getting into that room.

I had to stop for tea but I went straight back upstairs as soon as I'd finished. I was determined to get into the Diamond Den before I went to bed and I'd almost reached my target. I'd just started chatting to Pixie in the Emerald room when the screen changed suddenly.

"YOU'VE MADE IT, MARCIA MOON!" it said. "YOU HAVE 1000 POINTS."

I held my breath, waiting to see what would happen next. It had taken me so long to get to this point and I was desperate to know what was in the Diamond Den but I couldn't help feeling scared – as if in some way it was too late to turn back. And then the screen changed again. Everything disappeared and the only thing left was a door with a diamond handle. A new message flashed across the screen...

"BUT TO ENTER THE DIAMOND DEN YOU MUST COMPLETE ONE FINAL STEP."

The Final Step!

Congratulations, Marcia, you are one of the chosen few. Only SPECIAL people like you are granted access to the Diamond Den. To take up this rare opportunity you must pay £100 and enter the following details.

Full Name:

Address:

Date of Birth:

Name of Credit Card Holder:

Credit Card Number:

This is a one-off payment. You will not be asked for any more money. Your bank details will be safe with us. We will not share this information with anyone else.

Hurry, Marcia. You have only <u>one week</u> to pay.

Your time starts now.

A clock appeared on the screen and started to tick. The ticking seemed to grow louder until it was right inside my head. No one had mentioned paying money when I first logged on to the site and Skye had never said anything about it either. Filling in my name, address, and date of birth would be easy, but I didn't have a credit card and I certainly didn't have a hundred pounds.

I tried to reason with myself that my details would be safe. It's not like I was giving them out to some stranger in the Emerald room. And, anyway, I deserved to enter that room. I'd been chatting for so long and I'd earned so many points and it didn't seem fair that Skye had entered the room and left me behind.

The more I thought about it the more unfair it seemed. The more unfair *everything* seemed. I mean it wasn't really my fault that I'd let Mandy down so badly. The way I saw it, if Dad hadn't dumped Mum to move in with Diane, then Mum would never have moved to Spain and none of this would've happened in the first place. Basically, it was all *Dad's* fault: Mum leaving, Cosmo's accident and me losing my part at drama. And since *he* was to blame for everything, it was only fair that *he* should pay for me to enter the Diamond Den, wasn't it?

I sat there for ages just staring at the screen. The room grew cold around me. I didn't want to enter my personal details and I didn't want to steal money off Dad but I *did* want to get through that door more than anything. In the end I logged off and went to bed, but it was impossible to get to sleep. I tossed and turned all night going over everything that had happened. It was like I had a virus inside my head – whirling round and round, twisting everything up – until I didn't know what was right any more.

It was a terrible week. Phoebe kept nagging me to tell Mandy about Mum going to Spain and Cosmo's accident, but I knew it wouldn't make any difference; not now. She went on and on about it so much that in the end I told her to get lost.

Cosmo got more and more fed up with his plastic hood and I was convinced that the minute Mr. Adesina removed it he'd be straight back down to number 25. On Thursday, Mum called to say she wouldn't be able to get back for the show because she had a meeting she couldn't afford to miss, something to do with her promotion. She was really upset and she promised she'd make it up to me, but it was obvious her job was more important to her than her own daughter.

And every night I went to bed and thought about getting into the Diamond Den – I went over and over it until I thought my head was going to explode.

Friday night was the worst. I had to make my mind up by the next morning and I still didn't know what to do for the best. Obviously it would be really bad to take Dad's credit card, but I couldn't help feeling that somehow he *owed* me the money. I had never taken anything from anyone in my life but, for some reason, this felt different. I heard Jake wake up at one point, deep in the night, and I heard Diane soothe him back to sleep. I almost called out to her, to tell her *I* couldn't sleep; to ask her to soothe *me* back to sleep – but of course I didn't.

As soon as I got up on Saturday morning I knew what I was going to do. Dad and Diane were in the kitchen with Jake getting breakfast ready, so I had to act fast. I crept into their bedroom and started to rummage around in the drawer next to Dad's side of the bed. There was a book and one of Jake's yucky dummies and lots of receipts and things, but no credit card.

I looked around the room. My heart was thumping and I felt completely sick. I spotted a pair of trousers Dad had left lying across the bed. The pockets were heavy, jangling with keys and coins and I could feel the shape of his wallet in there too.

"Breakfast," Diane called up the stairs. "Come on, Polly. It's on the table."

My hands froze, clutching the trousers. "I'll be down in a sec," I squeaked. I shoved my hand into one of the front pockets, grabbed the wallet and scooted down the hall to my room.

There were quite a few cards to sort through: a supermarket loyalty card, a library card and a couple of others. His credit card was red and gold and it had a long number right across the middle. I slipped it under some papers on my desk, stuffed everything else back into the wallet, and then raced down the hall to Dad's room before I could change my mind.

"Morning, princess," said Dad as I walked into the kitchen. He handed me a glass of juice. "How do you fancy a day out? It's such gorgeous weather we thought we'd meet you straight from drama and find a lovely walk somewhere. We could take that picnic hamper you won at the dance contest. What do you think?"

"Sorry, Dad, I'm way too tired. I didn't sleep very well last night."

"Oh no! It wasn't because of Jake, was it?" said Diane. "Did you hear that, Jake?" she said, waggling her finger at the baby. "You've kept your big sister awake *again*."

Jake reached his arms out to me and tried to say Polly but it came out sounding more like poo and Dad and Diane burst out laughing.

I desperately wanted them to stop being so nice. It was almost as if they were doing it on purpose to make me feel guilty. But then I thought about Sam taking my part and how unfair it was and how *everything* was Dad's fault and I didn't feel half as bad.

"It wasn't because of Jake," I mumbled, sitting down at the table. "But I'm not going to drama today – I'm just too knackered."

Dad glanced at Diane. "What's up, Polly?" he said. "You can't keep missing drama when the show's so close. It's the dress rehearsal today, isn't it?"

"Look, have something to eat," said Diane, gently. "Your dad will drive you up there so you won't have to get the bus."

I trailed back upstairs with a slice of toast. It tasted like cardboard and the more I chewed it the harder it was to swallow. I dropped it in the bin and sat down at the computer. I took out Dad's credit card and typed in the long number. My fingers were trembling but it was like my brain had stopped working. I had to get inside that room and *nothing* was going to stop me; not Dad or Diane or baby Jake.

I lifted my hand up to press enter. The clock on the screen was ticking. It was so loud it seemed to fill the whole room. I lowered my finger towards the keyboard and was just about to enter the information when the doorbell rang.

I froze, my finger suspended over the key. The ticking seemed to get even louder. I heard a muffled voice I didn't quite recognize. And then feet pounding up the stairs. My bedroom door burst open.

"For goodness' sake, Polly, you're not even dressed! Come on! We've got to go!"

It was Sam!

"What are you talking about?" I stammered. I minimized the screen and slipped Dad's credit card back under the papers.

"It's the dress rehearsal and we're going to be late if we don't get a move on." She held my jeans out to me.

"I'm not going," I said, my heart thumping so loud I was sure she must be able to hear it. "And what are you doing here anyway?"

She sighed impatiently. "I've come to get *you*, silly!" She sounded just like Mum. "Phoebe and Monty B came round yesterday after school and they told me all about poor Cosmo."

I stared at her.

"Why didn't you tell me? I saw him just now with that awful plastic collar. Bella had to have one of those once and it nearly broke my heart. She absolutely hated it. Why didn't you tell me Cosmo had been run over and that's why you missed drama?"

I just stood there gawping. I didn't know what to say.

"Come on, don't just stand there! Get dressed! We've got to tell Mandy."

"Tell her what?"

She rolled her eyes as if I was completely stupid. "That you're Marcia, of course! And that I'm Cydore and Phoebe's Rainbow and Rachel's...well, Rachel's in the chorus because that's what she wanted in the first place."

"You mean you're giving me my part back?"

"Well, it's up to Mandy obviously but there's

no way *I'm* doing it – not now I know about Cosmo."

It was difficult to take in. I couldn't believe Phoebe had gone round to Sam and told her everything when I'd asked her not to. The last thing I wanted was Sam Carter feeling sorry for me. "Well I don't want the part just because my cat got run over," I said, folding my arms across my chest to show her how serious I was.

"What are you talking about, Polly? No one feels sorry for you, you've just been too upset to learn your lines and that's what we're going to tell Mandy – if we ever get there! Come *on!*"

So Phoebe had been right all along. She was just trying to be a good friend and I'd been so horrible to her. I'd told her to get lost and everything. And now Sam was here – standing in my bedroom – being nice, and caring, and *fair*. It was like I'd gone to sleep and woken up in some sort of alternative universe where everything was upside down. I didn't have a clue what Mandy would say when we got to drama but it had to be worth a try.

"So are you coming or not?" said Sam, grinning.

I grinned back. I couldn't help it. "Of course I'm coming. Just wait downstairs for a second while I get ready."

As soon as I heard her on the stairs I brought the screen back up on the computer. I still wanted to enter the Diamond Den but I couldn't think about it just then. I pressed the back key and all the details on the screen disappeared. The only thing left was the clock. It was ticking loudly and underneath it said, "You have only nine hours left to enter your personal details." I'd be back from drama by two so I'd still have four-and-a-half hours left to decide.

Downstairs, Sam was sitting on the sofa cuddling Cosmo and chatting away to Dad and Diane.

"My cat's called Bella, she's a Russian Blue – that's a pedigree, you know. She's very old now but I used to enter her in shows all the time and she *always* came first. She did her last show a few months ago. It was for older cats but she was still the most beautiful cat there."

I nearly burst out laughing. She was so bossy and such a show-off but it suddenly seemed funny more than anything else and I felt like giving her the biggest hug.

"Come on, Sam," I said. "My dad's going to drive us up to drama in his van."

Dad winked at me over Sam's head, and just as we left the house I heard Diane say, "Bella might be a Russian Blue, Cosmo, but we wouldn't swap you for the world."

20
ConVincing Mandy

When we got to drama Mandy was in a total panic. Apparently her computer had crashed right in the middle of printing the programmes.

"I know, I know, it's the most ridiculous thing ever! We're doing a show called CRASH! and my computer goes and dies on me just when I need it most."

"Can't you get the programmes printed at a proper printing shop?" Tara suggested.

Mandy ran her hand through her hair, sighing. "I wish I could, Tara, but it would cost a bomb. I want them printed in colour and we need about two hundred. Anyway, I can't waste any more time worrying about it right now.

Let's sort out the costumes and crack on."

Sam took me by the hand. "Come on, we'll ask her now."

"She'll never say yes," I said, pulling back. "She's in such a bad mood already, it's hopeless."

But Sam didn't take any notice, she just yanked me back towards Mandy as if I hadn't said a word.

"Oh, hello, girls," said Mandy, handing Sam her costume. "Can you believe what's happened? It's like my worst nightmare. Anyway, I've done a costume for you, Polly, it's under here somewhere." She started to rummage around in a big pile of virus costumes.

"Could we just talk to you about something, Mandy?" said Sam. Then she carried on without waiting for an answer. "You see, Polly's cat Cosmo was in a terrible accident. It was a hit and run. The driver didn't even hang around to see if there was anything he could do.

Polly had to carry him for miles to get help and he lost pints of blood and he only just survived after undergoing an emergency operation."

Mandy stopped sorting through the costumes and looked up.

"Anyway," Sam went on, "that's the reason she didn't learn her lines, it was all way too traumatic, but now she has learned them, so can we all go back to the parts we had before?"

"Oh, Polly. That's awful. Why didn't you let me know about your cat?"

I shrugged and looked down at the floor. It all seemed so silly now we were actually telling her.

"Well I'm not really happy about swapping the parts back at such a late stage..." She stopped and I held my breath, certain she was going to say no. "But I suppose I *should* give you one last chance, Polly, especially if you've been having such a bad time."

I felt like jumping up and down and

cheering. "Do you really mean it?"

"I do, but if you miss even one line today we'll have to change straight back. Give that costume to Polly, Sam, and I'll find the other one in a sec. And you'd better go and tell Phoebe and Rachel so they know what's going on."

"That's that then," said Sam. "All sorted."

I still couldn't get over how nice she was being. I kept expecting her to turn round and say "April Fool" or something, even though it was the middle of June.

Mandy handed Sam her costume and mask. "I'm really proud of you, Sam. Polly's so lucky to have such a good friend."

We went over to find the others and tell them what was going on. Phoebe was so happy she nearly burst into tears.

"That's amazing," she said. "I'm so pleased it's all worked out."

"Thanks to you and Monty B," I said. "I can't

believe you did that for me."

"Well you *are* my friend, Polly," she said. "Even if you act like a total idiot sometimes."

I stared at the floor, feeling a bit guilty. I hadn't been a very good friend to Phoebe at all over the last few weeks but I was determined to make it up to her. I gave her a hug and went off to find Rachel. She was happy as well. She said she'd been having nightmares about doing so many extra lines, especially as she'd never even been in a school play before, let alone a proper show like this one.

When everyone was ready, Mandy sat us down for a chat.

"Those of you who did the last show at Star Makers know that we have to treat this rehearsal like a proper performance. We can't stop and start like we did last week, we've got to run straight through. The next time we perform it will be in front of a packed audience, so we've got to get it right today."

I started to feel a bit nervous. I really didn't want to let her down.

"But you do all look fantastic," she added. "So I'll just take a few photos of you up on the stage and then we'll get going."

The set was amazing. Mandy's boyfriend, Julian, had made these giant circuit boards out of huge sheets of wood covered in bright green felt. He'd stuck old takeaway cartons and other bits and pieces onto the boards and sprayed them all metallic silver. There were rows of matches and small yoghurt pots and different-sized bottle tops all carefully arranged to look like wires and ports and cables. The boards were big enough to go all the way round the stage, so it looked as if we were actually inside a real computer.

We got into groups for the photos, depending on our character in the show. I was with Monty B and Sam was with all the other viruses. Phoebe had her photo by herself. Her costume was a rainbow-striped minidress with bright pink and purple tights and sparkly purple platforms – she looked so funky!

"So ze dream-team are togezer again," said Monty B when we went up onto the stage for our turn.

"Yeah, well, thanks for going round to Sam's. Phoebe did try to convince me I should tell her about my cat getting run over but I didn't think it would make any difference."

"Your cat!" snorted Monty B. "You think she changed her mind because of your cat?"

"Why did she change it then? What did you do – threaten her or something?"

"No! I just promised her that if we ever did another ballroom dance contest she could definitely be my partner. You don't think she was going to turn down an offer like that, do you?"

I burst out laughing and Mandy clicked the camera.

"Try to look a bit more frightened, Polly," she

called out. "It's not supposed to be a comedy!"

We had so much fun doing the photos that I forgot for a minute about proving to Mandy that I could do Marcia's part. I *had* practised at home, and with Phoebe at school, but that was last week, before Mandy had given the part to Sam. And anyway, acting out the lines in my bedroom or with Phoebe wasn't the same as doing it here in front of everyone else.

When all the photos were done we helped Mandy set the stage up ready for the opening.

"Okay, Polly," she said. "I want you to sit at Marcia's desk until I give you the signal to start. The rest of you need to wait offstage and I don't want to hear a sound."

Phoebe and the others squashed themselves into the wings, giggling and mucking about. I almost wished I could squash in there with them, but I had to sit all by myself at the desk and wait for Mandy.

"When you're ready, Polly," said Mandy, as

soon as the others were quiet.

But I wasn't ready and for one terrible moment the lines were gone. I couldn't even remember the first word. It was completely silent in the hall. Mandy sat at the piano, waiting. I so didn't want to mess it up but my mind was totally blank.

"We've really got to get going," said Mandy. She didn't sound cross but I could tell she was starting to lose patience.

It had all been such a rush coming to drama, what with Sam turning up and everything, that I'd totally forgotten to bring my script. I hadn't even looked at the lines since last Saturday. My palms started to sweat. I knew if I blew it today Mandy would give the part straight back to Sam.

"We're going to run out of time, Polly," said Mandy. "What's the problem?"

I looked across at Sam in the wings. She was mouthing something at me.

I shook my head to show her I didn't understand. It was a nightmare.

"It's so lonely sometimes," she hissed. "Stuck here in my room, day after day, all by myself."

And suddenly the words came flooding back, as if someone was holding the script up right in front of me. I grinned at Sam, wiped my hands on my jeans and started to speak. Once I'd got going, the rest of Act One was fine. Everyone remembered their lines, and when they were supposed to come on, *and* all the dance moves.

"That was fantastic," said Mandy, when we stopped for a break. "I can't believe how good it was. It was almost too good," she joked. "Something's bound to go wrong at some point."

But Act Two went just as well. It was so different from last term when our dress rehearsal had been a total disaster; mostly because Arthur had double-booked the hall and another group had turned up to rehearse *their* play at the same time.

"You guys are amazing," Mandy kept saying. "I can hear every word and it's so slick and professional."

When Phoebe came on to sing her big solo she looked scared out of her wits and, for a horrible second, I thought she was going to run straight back offstage.

Come on, Phoebs. You can do it, I said inside my head, and it was as if she could actually hear me. She took a deep, shaky breath, opened her mouth and started to sing. Her voice was beautiful. It seemed to fill every corner of the hall and I was so proud of her I felt like cheering.

We ran right through to the end with no problems at all and then we stopped to sort out the bows and the finale.

"Brilliant, Polly!" Mandy called out when I ran onstage with Monty B. "You were just brilliant!"

It was weird, but I'd hardly thought about the Diamond Den all morning and standing on the stage with everyone – singing the last song and having so much fun – it seemed totally crazy that I was even *thinking* of stealing from my own dad. It was as if the friend2friend website had taken over my brain in some way and I knew exactly what I was going to do the second I got home.

"You were great, Polly," said Sam when we'd finished the bows.

"So were you," I said. "I bet Mandy will give you the biggest part next time. And if she doesn't I'll have a word with her."

"We *all* will," said Phoebe.

Just then Arthur came in.

"Oh, hello, Mandy, my dear," he said. "Rehearsal going well?"

"Yes, thanks, Arthur," she said, smiling. "What can I do for you?"

He waved a bit of paper at her. "The piano

was delivered yesterday," he announced. "And Mr. Duke, the manager at the old people's home, has kindly sent through this picture on the computer. It's just marvellous, isn't it, the way we communicate these days? Anyway, we're all very grateful, so like I said the other week, if there's anything at all I can do to help…"

Mandy looked at the picture of the piano. "Well there is something," she said slowly. "I see you have a colour printer."

"Yes, it's a marvel, isn't it? Don't know how to work it myself but the lovely Mrs. Beagle is a whiz."

"Only I'm having a bit of trouble with *my* computer at the moment," said Mandy, "and I was right in the middle of printing out the programmes for our show. The thing is I've got so much to do and…"

"Say no more!" boomed Arthur, holding up his hand to stop Mandy. "Just give me the details and the job will be done."

"Are you sure that was a good idea?" said Catharine, after Arthur had skipped off back to his office, clutching a copy of the programme.

"I know what you mean," said Mandy. "But it's so straightforward, what could possibly go wrong?"

I couldn't wait to get home to tell Dad and Diane how well the rehearsal had gone – and that Mandy had agreed to let me be Marcia again. I hadn't actually told them I'd lost the part in the first place but I was suddenly bursting to tell them the whole story. I raced all the way back from the bus stop, thinking about the show and how great it was going to be, and how Mandy had said I was brilliant. I didn't even feel that upset about Mum not being there to watch me. I pulled the door key out of my pocket, but before I could get it into the lock, the door flew open from the inside.

It was Dad.

And he was holding his credit card.

21
Dad Finds Out

I suppose I could've lied. I could've said I was using the credit card to buy Diane a thank-you present for saving Cosmo's life. Or I could've got angry and demanded to know what Dad was doing in my room in the first place. I mean he is always going on about how it's *my private space* and stuff like that. But in the end I didn't lie or get angry. I just froze, with my eyes fixed on the card.

Dad grabbed my arm and yanked me into the lounge. "Right then," he said. "Perhaps you'd like to explain why my credit card was in your room? *And* why the computer says you only have a few hours left to enter your personal details?"

He was so angry he looked as if he was about to explode.

"It was just this w-website," I stammered. "And I needed your credit card to get into the... the...Diamond Den." It sounded so pathetic when I said it out loud.

Diane walked in from the kitchen. "What's going on?" she said.

"Polly has been using my credit card."

"No I haven't actually *used* it!" I cried. "I took it this morning but I didn't use it. I was going to give it back as soon as I got home, I swear."

"But why should I believe you?" Dad shouted. *"You've lied to me before so why should I believe you now? And how could you be so stupid? Don't you know how dangerous it is to give out your personal details on the computer? I thought you had a bit more sense than that!"*

Diane put her hand on his arm. "Calm down, Simon. Polly's trying to explain. Why don't you sit down together and talk it through? I'll go and make a cup of tea."

He shook off her hand. "A cup of tea's not going to make things right this time," he snapped. "You know, I'm sick to death of tiptoeing around her. Trying to understand. Giving her time to settle in. It's about time she started to grow up a bit and take some responsibility for her actions."

I'd never seen Dad this angry. Diane scooted out of the room and I shrank back in my seat.

"I'm sorry," I whispered. "I know it was wrong. I was just so caught up with this website and this friend I made and the more we chatted the harder it was to stop and it helped me feel better; you know, about Mum leaving and Cosmo and stuff like that, but I wasn't going to go on it any more and I'm not lying."

Dad started to pace around the room. He went round and round, his huge, muscly arms folded across his chest and it was obvious he wasn't calming down at all.

"Even if I decide to believe you about not going on the site again," he said, still pacing, "you need to understand just how serious it was to take my credit card and to enter your personal details onto the computer."

"But Dad, I *do* understand!"

"I want you to show me this website," he went on, ignoring me. "Don't you understand how dangerous it is? You have absolutely no idea who you've been talking to. You didn't arrange to *meet* anyone, did you?"

"Of course not!"

"It's my fault as well. I should've kept a closer eye on you. I knew it was stupid to let you have a computer in your bedroom. No more hiding away upstairs talking to a bunch of strangers. Are you listening, Polly?"

I nodded and started to get up from the sofa.

"Hang on a minute. I haven't finished." He started pacing again. I could see he was thinking up some awful punishment. He went round and round the living room. "I'm sorry, Polly," he said finally. "But as soon as I've sorted out the computer, I'm going to phone Mandy and tell her you won't be able to take part in the production."

My heart started to thud. "*What*? What do you mean? You can't do that. She's only just given me my part back!"

He swung round to face me. "I *can*, Polly. And that's exactly what I'm going to do. This is very serious. You were going to *steal* from me."

"*But that's so unfair. I'll be letting everyone down. I don't care what else you do to me – but not that! Why do you always have to ruin everything?*"

"She's right, Simon," said Diane, coming back into the room. "She can't let everyone else down just because she's done something she shouldn't. I know she took your credit card but she says she didn't use it and I believe her."

"This is none of your business! She's not even your daughter!" Dad roared at Diane, and then he stormed out of the room.

I started to cry. It was horrible. I'd never seen him shout at Diane.

"Don't worry, Polly," she said. "I'll talk to him. Pop up to your room for a bit."

I ran upstairs and threw myself on the bed. I could hear Dad and Diane arguing. Their voices grew louder and louder – Dad's especially. After a bit I went over to the computer and unplugged it. I didn't even close it down properly, I just ripped the plug out of the wall. I didn't care about Skye or the Diamond Den or anything to do with the friend2friend website. I just wanted Dad to stop shouting.

At some point Jake woke up from his afternoon nap and started to cry. I went into his room and picked him up out of his cot. He was clutching hold of Boo and his face was all crumpled and tear-stained. "It's all right," I said. "Polly's here now." He clung on to me, burying his face in my neck. I managed to keep him happy for a bit, dancing Boo around the edges of the cot and making silly noises, but he was starving and in the end I carried him downstairs to Diane.

She was sitting on her own in the lounge. Her face was all crumpled up like Jake's and I could see she'd been crying.

"What's happened, Diane? Where's Dad?"

"It's okay, Polly, he's just popped out to get some fresh air. I've persuaded him to wait until tomorrow before he calls Mandy. I think he's more frightened about what could have happened than anything. And cross with himself."

Dad came up to my room a bit later. He sat on the end of my bed and I told him everything.

About pretending to be Marcia and making friends with Skye and how chatting to her helped me to forget about Mum and how much I was missing her. He didn't interrupt or stop listening halfway through, like he usually does, and when I'd finished he took me in his arms.

"I'm so sorry, princess," he said. "I just didn't realize what a difficult time you were having. You kept on saying you were fine but I should've paid more attention. And you know, this friend of yours, Skye. Well, she's not a real friend, sweetheart. She was probably just chatting to you to draw you into the site and get you to spend lots of money."

"I know," I whispered, "and I'm sorry as well. I'm sorry I took your credit card. I didn't know what I was doing. I just kept thinking that if I could get inside that room and talk to Skye again all my problems would be solved. And then I realized that I didn't even care about the Diamond Den any more, that I was happy at drama and that my real friends were so much more important than some stranger I'd never even met. I was on my way home to put back your credit card, but it was too late because you'd already found it in my room."

"It's not too late," Dad said. "I'm not going to stop you doing your show. But you do need to trust me more and I definitely need to listen to you more. Right now though, I think I'd better go down and beg Diane to forgive me for flying off the handle like that."

"Will you say thank you from me?" I said.

He shook his head. "No, you come down and tell her yourself. She'd appreciate that."

But I still didn't want to. There were all sorts of things I knew I *should* say to Diane like, *Thank you for saving Cosmo,* and, *Thank you for getting Dad to listen,* but I just couldn't.

So Dad didn't call Mandy and I spent the rest of the week going over my lines just to make absolutely sure I knew them inside out.

On Wednesday we took Cosmo to the vet to have his stitches removed – *and* the plastic hood. I thought he'd be straight back down to number 25 once he could fit through the cat flap again, but he seemed perfectly happy to stay where he was and, when I got home from school on Thursday, he was sitting on the wall outside number *11* waiting for a cuddle.

On Saturday morning Diane made pancakes for breakfast.

"It's just my way of saying good luck," she said.

"It's weird but I'd totally forgotten how much I love them," I said, helping myself to seconds. Diane looked chuffed to bits.

I knew it was the perfect moment to thank her for everything she'd done but, just as I was working out what to say, the phone rang. It was Mum calling to wish me luck. I didn't tell her about the credit card or anything. I just said I was feeling much happier and much more settled. She was thrilled and said that even though she couldn't watch me perform she'd be thinking about me every second of the day.

Phoebe arrived straight after breakfast and Dad drove us up to drama in the van.

"Hello, you two," said Mandy, as we walked through the doors. "You haven't seen Arthur, have you? He was supposed to be delivering the programmes first thing."

Mandy looked amazing. She'd dyed her hair again, for the first time in ages. It was jet black with fluorescent green tips, to match the virus costumes.

"Wow!" breathed Phoebe. "I *love* your hair. But no we didn't see Arthur, did we, Polly?"

I shook my head.

"I really hope he's remembered," she sighed. "I've tried calling him but he's not answering his phone."

We went backstage to get ready. Nearly

everyone was there sorting out their costumes and make-up. It was incredibly hot and noisy.

"You haven't seen my mask, have you?" asked Ellie. "I swear I left it right by all my stuff but I can't find it anywhere."

"Have you been to the toilet or anything?" Phoebe asked.

"The toilet!" Ellie cried, and she dashed off in the direction of the loos.

"I've been to the loo about fifty times," moaned Rachel. "I'm so nervous I swear I'm going to throw up any minute now."

"You'll be okay, Rachel," I said. "Everyone gets nervous when it's their first show."

"Except for me," said Monty B.

"I meant normal people actually," I said, "and I'm warning you – don't start adding any lines or doing anything stupid."

"Me? Do something stupid?" he said. Then he grabbed hold of me and started waltzing me round the tiny changing room.

Mandy popped her head round the door. "Not now, you guys," she said.

"Sorry, Mandy, Polly can't help herself," said Monty B. "She just finds me totally irresistible."

"In your dreams," I said, but I couldn't help grinning like an idiot.

There was just about enough time for one final run-through before the matinee was due to start. We were supposed to be practising Cydore's big scene, *with* the smoke machine, but Mandy couldn't find the right lead to hook it up.

"Can you actually believe it?" she said. "They've delivered the machine with three different leads and not one of them fits! Anyway, don't worry, Sam, Julian's sorting it out so we'll definitely have it in time for the first performance at three o'clock. It's not ideal, I know, but as long as no one starts coughing it'll be fine."

Tara started to cough and we all laughed.

"Just the thought of the stage filled with smoke makes me feel wheezy," she moaned.

"Tara, it's not real smoke," said Mandy. "Trust me."

We were just coming on to practise the bows when Arthur turned up with the programmes.

"Here they are, Mandy, and so sorry for the delay. I'll lay them out on the chairs, shall I? I can see how busy you are."

"Oh, that would be great! Thanks so much, Arthur."

"I'll give you a hand," said Catharine, jumping down off the stage.

Arthur clutched the programmes to his chest. "No, no, no," he spluttered, stepping back. "Stay right where you are. You carry on with your rehearsal and leave this to me."

"It's okay," said Mandy. "We've more or less finished anyway."

Catharine tried to take a pile of programmes out of Arthur's hands, but he held on to them as if his life depended on it. He was so desperate to keep them away from her that he didn't notice one single programme flutter down to the floor.

"Oh my God, yeah," said Neesha, leaping off the stage and picking it up. "You know what you said about how things were going too well, Mandy?"

"Yes," said Mandy, not even trying to smile.

"Well, Star Makers Drama Club is putting on a show called TRASH!"

22
Playing My Part At Last

"Now, Mandy, let me explain," said Arthur, trying to back out of the room.

"*What do you mean, explain?*" hissed Mandy, her face turning a deep red. "You have called my show *Trash!* The audience will be here in about fifteen minutes' time and they're going to think I'm putting on a show about computers called *Trash!* What are you going to explain exactly?"

Arthur took another step back. "It's just that Mrs. Beagle was off with a cold, but she very kindly offered to do the programmes at home. I read the details out to her over the phone but unfortunately the cold must have caused her ears to become a little blocked and it seems she misheard me."

"Mrs. Beagle *again*," said Mandy, faintly.

"It's easily done," said Arthur, stroking his beard. A big lump of something like cheese fell to the floor. "You see 'C' does sound like 'T' if your ears are blocked. You try it." He motioned for Mandy to put her fingers in her ears and we all started to giggle.

"Block your ears up like this and I'll say 'C' and you see how easy it is to mistake it for a 'T'."

"I'll tell you what the mistake was," cried Mandy. "The mistake was asking *you* to help in the first place. I mean *Trash!* You've called my show *Trash!*"

"Don't worry, Mandy," said Monty B. "I'll have a quick word with the audience. I'll explain all about Mrs. Beagle's blocked ears. I'll say 'T' is the new 'C'. I'll even sing a song if you want…" He trailed off and Arthur took the opportunity to bolt out of the door.

"*Trash!*" Mandy shouted after him. "It was

all going so well and now my show is called *Trash!*" She shook her head. "How on earth am I going to sort this out before the audience arrives?"

She shooed us backstage and the minute the door closed behind us we all burst out laughing. I think it must've been nerves.

"I told her not to trust him," spluttered Catharine. "The programmes were looking so good and now they're ruined."

"Did you see?" said Adam. "He actually thought Mandy was going to put her fingers in her ears while he said 'C' and 'T'."

Ellie groaned. "Don't," she said. "I won't be able to stop laughing and we're going on in a sec."

We were still talking about it when Mandy popped back to say the audience were coming in.

"Okay, calm down and get yourselves together. I'll go out and explain about the programmes but you guys really need to focus on your performance. Are you ready, Polly? I want you to stand in the wings with everyone else and as soon as I give you the signal, walk onto the stage and sit at Marcia's desk. Got that?"

I nodded. I didn't feel scared at all any more; I was just dying to show Mandy how well I could do.

"Good luck, Polly," said Sam.

"Yes, good luck, Princess Polly," said Monty B.

"You'll be brilliant," said Phoebe.

"I can't find my mask," wailed Ellie, and we all burst out laughing again.

The matinee went really well. It was noisy and chaotic, with heaps of children in the audience, but I didn't fluff any of my lines and Monty B didn't do anything stupid and we got a massive cheer for our dance. I loved being Marcia. It was so exciting to have such a big part and I couldn't wait to do it all over again in the evening.

The scene where Cydore replicates herself was incredible. Julian had managed to find the right lead for the smoke machine and when Sam started her eerie chant the stage filled with a thick, swirly white mist. It was so creepy the way the smoke seemed to fill the entire hall as the viruses appeared one after the other, all identical to Sam, and all chanting "ONE AND THEN ANOTHER, WE COPY EACH OTHER", over and over. The smoke kept pouring out until Phoebe came on to sing her solo – as if her goodness had literally cleared away the mist.

"Well done, everyone," cried Mandy afterwards, when she came backstage. "Especially you, Tara, for not coughing in Sam's big scene – which was amazing by the way."

"I actually held my breath all the way through," said Tara. "I thought I was going to die!"

"Well at least if you were dead, yeah, you wouldn't be able to cough," said Neesha.

Mandy came over and gave me a hug. "I'm so proud of you, Polly, you were fantastic. And Phoebe, oh my goodness, the hairs were standing up on the back of my neck – your song was incredible."

"Hey, what about me?" said Monty B. "Have I turned invisible or something?"

"Sadly not," said Adam. "But keep trying."

In the break between performances I went out for a snack with Phoebe and her family. Sara went on and on about the show – going through each character one by one. "You were the best, Polly," she said. "And Sam was really creepy. And I can see why you're all so crazy about that new boy Sandeep. He actually winked at me at one point."

"In your dreams," said Phoebe.

"Oh and your song was quite good as well, Phoebs," Sara went on. "You weren't actually singing in tune or anything, but at least you managed to get the words out this time."

"Just ignore her," I said to Phoebe, grinning. "I thought your song was amazing."

"And I'll tell you the weirdest thing of all," said Sara. "Last term you said you couldn't *stand* Polly and now you're like *best friends*."

Phoebe and I looked at each other and burst out laughing. She *was* my best friend. She was the best friend I'd ever had in my life.

Back at the hall, Mandy was going through each programme one at a time trying to turn the "T"s into "C"s. "Just remind me next term, *please*, never, *ever* to ask that man to do anything for me again."

We gave her a hand with the programmes and then went backstage to get ready.

Ellie was there frantically looking for her mask. "I don't know what's going on," she wailed. "I had it. I definitely had it. It's like I'm cursed or something!"

"Erm...Ellie... It's *on* your face!" said Phoebe.

"What?"

"You're wearing it!"

We all collapsed laughing as Ellie put her hand up to her face and then slumped against the wall in relief.

"My dad totally loved the set," said Sam, checking her make-up was okay in the mirror. "He thought the circuit boards were so realistic."

"What about your mum?" I said. "Is she coming tonight?"

"No, she can't. She's working. Well, that's what she said anyway."

"My mum's not coming either," I said, and I gave her a quick hug.

We chatted about our mums for a bit and then Mandy popped her head round the door to let us know that we only had ten minutes. The hall soon filled up and the atmosphere was electric. Julian had found this eerie computer music and it was playing through the speakers as the audience came in.

Just before we were due to go on I peeked through the curtain to see if Dad and Diane and Jake had arrived. I'd managed to get the last two tickets. Mandy had saved them for me just in case I changed my mind. I couldn't see them at first; there were so many people and the lights were dimmed, but then I spotted them – right in the middle, near the front. They were reading the programme, laughing at the front cover.

I stood there watching them for a bit. It still felt weird to see my dad sitting with Diane instead of with Mum, but not in a bad way. At one point Diane looked up and when she saw me peeking she waved like mad and mouthed *good luck*.

"Is your brother here?" said Monty B, coming up behind me. "Because I hope he realizes he can't be the centre of attention *every* time!"

Of course the second the curtain opened and Jake spotted me sitting at the desk, he started to squeal and bounce about, trying to get down from Diane's lap, but I didn't mind at all. I couldn't smile at him or wave or anything because I was supposed to be really sad and lonely – but I was smiling inside.

It was a brilliant performance, perfect really; I didn't want it to end. The audience went crazy, clapping and cheering when we came on for our bows, and I could see Diane holding Jake up while he clapped along with everyone else, his podgy little legs kicking like mad. Mandy made a lovely speech about how hard we'd worked and what a fantastic group we were. We sang "CRASH!" one more time and then it was all over.

It was chaos backstage. Everyone was trying to get changed and take photos of each other and get their programmes signed. Ellie couldn't find any of her stuff anywhere and was chucking things all over the place.

"Well done, guys!" cried Mandy, coming backstage. "You really did me proud. It's been the most amazing day. Go home for a well-deserved rest and next week we'll have a massive party to celebrate."

"Three cheers for Mandy!" Monty B shouted suddenly. And I cheered and cheered until I was hoarse.

"Polly Carter!" said Dad, when I came back out into the hall. "You were fantastic!" He wrapped his arms round me and squeezed me tight. "And I've got some wonderful news, princess," he said. "Your mum called again just before we left and she's managed to get next weekend off to fly back and see you. She was so gutted about not being here tonight."

"That's okay," I said, blushing a bit. I looked over at Diane and Jake and took a deep, shaky breath. "I've got the rest of my family here and they're just as important."

Diane's eyes filled with tears. "Thank you, Polly," she said. "I'm so proud of you."

"So am I," said Dad. "So proud I could burst."

Mandy was right. We do waste an awful lot of energy wishing our lives were different, or searching for something, instead of enjoying what's right in front of us.

"Can I have a cuddle with my gorgeous brother then?" I said to Jake, holding my hands out to take him from Diane. And Jake flung his arms round my neck and blew the biggest raspberry ever.

Read on for a sneak preview of the next brilliant Star Makers Club story...

Sam in the Spotlight

Why has Sam's sister fallen out with their mum? Will Dad ever reveal his secret from the past? How can Sam get her family back on track? And, most importantly, will she hold it all together on the night of Star Makers' fab new musical?

Sam in the Spotlight

My favourite book ever when I was a little girl was *Green Eggs and Ham* by Dr. Seuss. Not because I like weird food or anything but because of the opening lines: *I am Sam. Sam I am.* I bet I thought Dr. Seuss had written it just for me! My big sister Crystal used to read it to me over and over until I knew every word by heart. We would cuddle up together on my bed, with my beautiful kitten Bella, and I'd join in with all the rhymes. And then when I learned to read by myself, I would read it out loud to Mum – or Dad or Aunty Mags – or anyone else who was willing to listen.

Crystal says I used to wear this silly red hat just like Sam in the book and whenever she read it to me I would always shout out the words, "I am Sam! Sam I am!" as if I was the most important person in the world.

I actually found my old copy of *Green Eggs and Ham* today, stuffed at the back of my bookshelf. I was sure I'd given it away years ago, to a school jumble sale or something, but there it was squashed between my Oxford dictionary and one of my Jacqueline Wilson books.

I took it down off the shelf and wiped away the dust. I'd read it so many times the pages were almost furry; all soft and curled up at the edges. Just inside the front cover was a photo.

It was of me, Crystal and Bella – all sitting on my bed – reading *Green Eggs and Ham*.

I stared and stared at the photo. I'm wearing my little red hat just like Crystal said and I've got this look of total happiness on my face. Crystal's got her arm round me and she's laughing into the camera, her eyes sparkly and bright. *Crystal by name and Crystal by nature,* Dad always used to say. She must've been about eight in the picture but she already looks so grown-up for her age.

I rushed downstairs to show Mum. I don't know why but I just wanted her to see how happy we were. I burst into the living room shouting, "I am Sam! Sam I am!" like I was three again. Mum glanced up from her ironing and gave me a tight smile.

"Hey, look what I found," I said, holding the photo up to show her. "It's me in my silly red hat, remember?"

"What do you think you're doing, Sam?"

She snatched the photo out of my hand and turned it face down on the ironing board. "I thought you said you were sorting your things out for school."

"I know I was, but then I came across my old *Green Eggs and Ham* book and this photo was stuck inside, and it just got me thinking about Crystal and..." I trailed off.

Mum hates it when I talk about Crystal. She left home about four months ago, the day after her eighteenth birthday, and ever since then I only have to mention her name and Mum goes off on one.

"This is all part of your problem," she grumbled, waving the iron about in the air. "I send you upstairs to do one simple job and two seconds later you've got caught up doing something completely different. That's what your teachers keep saying, isn't it? That you can't concentrate."

"No they don't." I picked up the photo and

started backing out of the door. "Who actually said that? Who said I can't concentrate?"

Mum set the iron down, sighing heavily. "Look the point is, Sam, you're going into Year Eight and you're a clever girl. It's time to knuckle down and show us what you're capable of, isn't it, Dave?" She looked over at my dad. He was sitting across the room with Bella on his lap, reading the paper and humming the same tune over and over. He's been funny since Crystal left as well. It's like he's there but not there. I could probably dance around the room wearing a black bin liner, with a bucket on my head, and he still wouldn't look up.

Mum strode over to him and pulled the paper down. "Dave! Are you even listening to me? I was just saying..."

I took the opportunity to slip out of the room. When Mum got in a mood like that she could easily go on all night.

Next morning at breakfast she picked straight up where she'd left off. I hadn't even poured my cereal before she started going on about my grades and my homework and my A-tti-tude. That's her favourite word at the moment – *Attitude* – and according to Mum, mine's all wrong!

It's ever since Crystal left. Ever since she turned down a place at one of the top universities in the country and moved in with her low-life boyfriend – Mum's words by the way, not mine! Just because Crystal didn't want to follow the path Mum had carved out for her, she'd decided to turn all her attention on me.

"I know you think I'm going on, Sam, but I just want you to make something of yourself, that's all." She handed me a glass of juice. "Anyway, I've got a big delivery at work so I'm going up to get ready. As soon as you've eaten I want you to finish sorting out your room."

I sat there nibbling on my toast. I don't know what Mum thought I was going to do exactly when I left school. It's not like I was going to be a brain surgeon or some sort of physics professor. The only thing I've ever wanted to do is to be on the stage. I was still sitting there thinking about my glittering future as a **Broadway Star** when there was a knock on the back door and Aunty Mags burst in.

"Hello, gorgeous," she said, throwing her bag down and giving me a big kiss. "Any chance of a cuppa?"

Aunty Mags is Dad's sister and we're really close. She only lives about two streets away and she's always popping in to see me. I flicked the switch on the kettle and took down a mug. "My mum's in a mood," I said. "She thinks I'm going to be a brain surgeon or something."

Aunty Mags giggled. "She's just worried about you, Sam. You know what she's like. Where's Dad?"

"He's already left for work. That's all he does these days. Work work work! Hey you couldn't have a word with my mum, could you?" I clasped my hands together under my chin. "Please, Aunty Mags. For me. She's just upstairs getting ready."

"Well I'll try," she said slowly, popping a slice of bread in the toaster. "But she won't thank me for interfering."

I love my Aunty Mags so much. She's only a few years younger than Dad, but she's always up for a laugh. Even when things go wrong she still manages to see the funny side. She poured another cup of tea for Mum, plonked everything on a tray and disappeared upstairs.

I waited for a few minutes and then followed her up. I didn't really expect mum to listen to Aunty Mags but I was desperate. I could just about hear her voice through the door. She was telling Mum that it was time to give me a bit more freedom and let me make my own mistakes. That she couldn't live my life for me. I leaned in even closer, dying to hear what Mum would say to that – but just then my phone began to ring. It was my best friend Ellie, back from her holiday in France.

"Come straight over!" she squealed down the phone. "I've got so much to tell you!"

"What? What's going on? Tell me now!"

"No, I can't! Just get over here!"

I popped my head round the door to ask Mum if I could go and they both stopped talking in that really obvious way – like when you know you've interrupted some big secret.

To find out what happens next, read...

Star Makers Club

Sam in the Spotlight

Seriously good stuff. (Says me.)

Anne-Marie Conway

ISBN: 9781409521419

Coming soon...

Hi guys,

I grew up dreaming about being on the stage.
I joined a drama club and spent every spare
moment singing and dancing — convinced I was
going to be a star.

But at secondary school I began to feel shy
about performing. I lost a lot of confidence and
for the first time I wasn't sure if my dream to be
on stage would come true.

Years later I started up my own drama club,
Full Circle. I guess it was a way of keeping my
dream alive. I found that running a drama club
was as brilliant as performing myself — all the
same nerves and excitement!

One day I started to scribble down some ideas
for a book about a group of characters who join
a drama club. I called it Star Makers. There was
Phoebe who was very shy but could sing like an

angel and Polly who just wanted everything to stay the same, Sam the big show-off who was desperate to be a serious actress, and Monty B who liked to clown around. I'd created a special place where everyone is different but everyone has their moment to shine.

This is Polly's story and it's for everyone going through a change – new school, new friendships, new home. Changes are tough and scary, but it's Polly's friends at Star Makers who help her to see that they can be so exciting too.

I still have BIG dreams – but these days they're much more about writing than about singing and dancing.

Dreams are so important...I hope all of yours come true!

Anne-Marie x

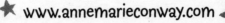
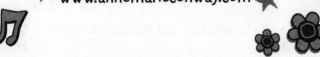
www.annemarieconway.com

'A warm, wise and
wonderfully witty read'
Cathy Cassidy

Why won't Phoebe's annoying neighbour,
Monty B, leave her alone? Can she get
her dippy dad and over-worked mum back
together again? Will class mean-girl, Polly
Carter, just get off her case for once? And
most important of all – will she overcome her
stage fright in time to sing her musical solo?

A warm-hearted story about the triumphs and
traumas at the Star Makers Drama Club – a special
place where everyone has their moment to shine!